Pounding The Pavement

A Novel by Nisha Lanae

Also by Nisha

Dice The Queen of Murder

Pounding the Pavement, A novel written by Nisha Lanae, Copyright 2013 by Nisha Lanae

Library of Congress Control Number 2013918872
ISBN-13: 978-0-615-99961-6
ISBN-10: 0615999611

Cover Designer: Brittani Williams
Editor: Tyresha Tyler

Dedications

I dedicate this to any and every woman young or old, who has struggled with Prostitution, low self-esteem or lack of knowing their own self-worth. I've never struggled with Prostitution, but I know a few who have. I've struggled with self-esteem issues and not long ago did I found my own self-worth. Remember love starts with self.

Acknowledgments

I have to give the most praise to the man upstairs, my father GOD, and my guardian angels. Without them I'm nothing. They have kept me, when depression wanted to take me under.

Book #2 yes baby lol, I'm so excited about this, it wasn't easy, but nothing worth it ever is.

To my parents, Thank You for giving me life, giving me a reason to go hard for my dreams and goals. Tara West (mom) you can't live in the past of what you didn't do while we were growing up, that's dead and gone, we have to live in the now and present and make that right. Warren Williams (Daddy) this year has passed so fast, I miss you dearly. You knew you were sick, and didn't want us to worry, so you held it in. Some days are better than others, but I know you wouldn't want me to cry, so I remember that and smile. To my younger siblings Travina & Tyrell I love you with all my heart and only want the best, even when I am flipping out. To my niece Kilee G, when I look into your eyes, I know you're a gift from God.

To the many women who have come into my life, leaving me with gems about love, life and respect for self. I am truly grateful for you all. Henrietta Binford, Latrice Lewis, Wanda Trotter and the Davis family, Cynthia Clark and all of my aunties. Regina Bullard, from the beginning you have had my back, and you still do, today. Thanks for helping my father all those years with me, my brother and sister we love you auntie.

To my love, my ace, my shoulder to lean on, my friend Dominic Funtila. Thanks for loving me for who I am, and pushing me, when I fell short, I love ya'.

Last but never least, I thank my readers and supporters and friends, without you there is no me, and what I love to do. Thanks for embracing me as a new Author. Thanks to the numerous Authors, who have given me advice, and wisdom on this writing and publishing journey. I have learned so much, and still have so much to learn.

Much, Much Thanks to the ladies of JS Promotion, you ladies rock, you go so hard for me and all of the other Authors you promote. If you need Promotions find them on Facebook.

Thanks you for purchasing this book, I hope you are intrigued with this story.

Much Love Nisha Lanae

Don't forget to find me on your favorite social network.

Facebook Nisha Lanae

Instagram Pendiva_Williams

Email Author.nishalanae@yahoo.com

Website www.NishaLanae.com

I didn't choose this life, this life choose me. I am the offspring of a Pimp and a Madam.

-Kandiland

Prologue

It was 3am when I was awaken out of my sleep, drenched in sweat and breathing hard, I was having a minor panic attack, and I had been having the same dream for the last month. It was my twin brother Kris and I, we were committing murder. It was the faces that were looking back at us that scared me the most; it was us. Kris and I with a loaded berretta pointed at our own heads. It felt like we were looking in the mirror battling ourselves with life and committing our own death.

I sat up in the bed I shared with my husband Monty, who lay next to me still sound asleep. I glanced over at the clock on the nightstand. It was the anniversary of a murder I would never forget; the night I killed my parents. It had been five years since I emptied the clip into their bodies. Nobody ever questioned their whereabouts or even reported them missing. In the wicked lifestyle they took part in anyone was a suspect, but they were nowhere on the priority list of missing people or victims. I got out of bed and went into the bathroom and ran a cold shower to wash the sweat from my sticky body. After finishing my shower I wrapped the plush robe around my body and made my way down the hallway to check on my children. I peeped in to see my 2-year-old son Karter, and 1-year-old daughter Kaila, curled up in Karter's bed asleep. I had to smile they were inseparable; they were the best gift life had offered me. I didn't know what I did to deserve such a blessing with the fucked up cards life had dealt me, or the lives I destroyed to get to this point. Seeing them smile made me feel that life wasn't so bad for me and I had been given another chance for a reason unknown to me. I closed the door halfway and put the video baby monitor into my robe pocket and made my way down the stairs to the kitchen. I poured me a glass of lemon water took two of the Diazepam pills that sat on the counter into my mouth. I grabbed the latest issue of Sister 2 Sister magazine and sat on the sofa and flipped through the pages and reflected on my life and how I got to this place where I was at now; I was a wife and mother. If anyone would have asked me 5 years ago where would I be today? I would have told them to stay out mine because the only thing that I was taught was to make a nigga cum fast, collect the cash, and onto the next. It was a hoe's motto; nothing else mattered besides chasing the almighty dollar.

"Kandi, Kandi, wake up babe" I heard Monty voice. I looked up to see him and the kids standing in front of me, still in their PJs. I had to smile at the sight; it was lovely.

"Hey, I must have fallen asleep down here while I was reading, what does everyone want for breakfast?"

"I want pancakes mommy," Karter said.

"Okay, let mommy go wash her face and brush her teeth and pancakes are coming up."

I hurried upstairs to handle my business so I could make my family a healthy breakfast before we started our day.

After making breakfast and getting the kid's dressed, I made Monty's lunch for work. I had to drop the kids off at my brothers. Today was the first day I was going to see a Psychologist for the first time in my life. I couldn't keep letting the past and the hurt I suffered to continue to be an issue for me. I wanted to move forward and I had to get my past off my chest, to stop carrying the burden inside so I could have a future. So my husband could have a wife; and my children could have a mother. I was tired of hiding from my past; today I was taking a step in releasing all of the dirt, pain and anguish from my past.

"What time do you meet with the Psychologist, Kandi?"

"I'm headed there right after I drop the kid's off"

"Well how do you feel about it? Are you okay? Do you want me to go with you?" I smiled as Monty rambled all the questions off, without taking a breath.

"It's something I have to do, to better me, and no, I got it. You just go to work, I will call you when I'm done."

"Okay, well call me if you change your mind, I'm only a phone call away."

"I know, I got it, enjoy your day."

"I will, you do the same, I love you."

"I love you too!"

I kissed my husband and knew I had to do this, I needed to be a better wife to him and a better mother to our children; they deserved it. I got the kids together and was on my way to start my day.

I dropped the kids off to my brother's house, his wife usually watched the kids for me. I then hopped back into my car and made my way towards the Psychologist office in Beverly Hills. Dr. Gwen was known for her star-studded clientele, she was the best in the business. As I walked to the large building, a sense of relief came over me. *"I'm doing this for my family"* I said to myself, while walking into the office building.

"Welcome to the office of Dr. Gwen, do you have an appointment today?" the receptionist asked.

"Yes, Kandi Jackson, I have a ten o'clock appointment with Dr. Gwen."

"Okay Mrs. Jackson take a seat, I will let her know you are here."

"Thank you," I said to her as I found a seat in the waiting area. I grabbed a magazine and flipped through it while I waited.

"Mrs. Jackson," I heard someone call out.

"Yes, I'm Mrs. Jackson."

I was slightly taken back by Dr. Gwen, she looked young, like she was only a few years older then me. Life had aged her very well.

"Right this way with me, I'm Dr. Gwen."

"Hello Dr. Gwen, you know who I am," I laughed nervously.

"Do you mind if I call you, Kandi?"

"Sure."

"Okay Kandi, where would you like to start?"

"In order to know why I am here, I guess the beginning"

"Okay, I'm listening," Dr. Gwen said as she took the seat across from me and grabbed her note pad.

Chapter 1

"I didn't choose this life, I was born into this fucked up life".

Many looked down on women who sold their self for the almighty dollar; prostitution is one of the oldest professions known. Many felt it was a disgrace to use your body as a form of making money. God's Temple, was reserved for one husband, not several men. Inquiring minds wanted to know what could go so wrong in your life that would make you hit rock bottom to solicit your body in exchange for money. Let alone give it to a man, your Daddy, your pimp. I'm here to tell you not everyone choose this life, yeah some have, others let their love for a man put them there; then you have me, who was born into the wicked lifestyle of Prostitution. Since I was conceived my destiny had been set for me, my parent's made the decision upon my mother finding out she was with child. That whatever they brought into this world, would be the new generation of the Timmons family. I'm one of the off springs of a Madam and a Pimp.

My estranged parents Erica and Paul, were beyond ecstatic to find out that they were expecting twins. 1 boy and 1 girl, on September 23rd 1990 on a warm day in Southern California they gave birth to Kris and me. We were the newest addition to the Timmons family, and its building empire.

The first time I can remember going on an outing with The Madam, my mother Erica; I had to be five.

"Madam, why do I always have to wear dresses? I see the other girls and they wear pants like Kris and Big."

"Because you are gonna' be a lady. Ladies always wear sexy dresses and nice skirts. They are easy access and they embrace your womanly curves. Only gay women wear pants like men, and make sure you always keep a clean toodah and smell good. A stank ass toodah isn't going to get you anything, but a trip to the doctors office and a meal from McDonalds."

"But I like McDonalds Madam."

"That's because you're still a child, when you get my age you are not going to want that bullshit. You are going to want to dine at all the fancy five star restaurants. A woman with a funky toodah doesn't get treated to those kinds of places."

"Okay," I replied. I was young, innocent and believed The Madam couldn't steer me wrong so I sat back in the chair. Every Tuesday we came to the same hotel room and spent hours there, just The Madam and me.

"Now you know the rules, no talking to anyone you don't know and you don't move, unless I say so, or Big comes," The Madam said as she went into the room with the man who walked through the door. Like always I knew there would be more. I sat back with my toys and entertained myself.

Big would come every once in awhile and bring me food. Today he hadn't come; I was hungry and bored of playing with my baby doll. I got up to walk around; I jumped from a sound that I heard from the door. I ran back to my seat, the same seat I always occupied when we came. Two of Madam friends walked in, just as the other one who had been in the room with her was leaving, I looked at the men some of them came every week while some I had never saw. The hours passed slow I was parched and hungry, but I couldn't interrupt The Madam, last time I got into trouble I couldn't sit down for two days after Big was done whipping me with his open bare hand.

Just as my eyes were about to give out on me, Big walked his husky frame through the door. I wanted to tell him I was thirsty and hadn't eaten, but he always yelled. I waited patiently; hoping Madam brought it up.

Madam peaked out the room and saw that Big was there, she went back into the room, and then emerged with a bag. She threw the bag to Big.

"Give me 15 more minutes" Madam went back into the room; she still had one of her friends inside.

Big spilled the content onto the floor in front of us, the bag was filled with money. Big started counting the money, a wide grinned formed on his face as he got down to the end of the crumbled up money.

"Today has been a great day Baby Girl," Big said rubbing his hands together. He pulled one of the bills from the stack. "You see this?" he asked me holding up the bill.

"Yes" I replied.

"If a man can't give you bills with Ben Frank on it, you don't need to be fuckin' with him." Big said handing me the hundred dollar bill. "That's for you, if a nigga say he don't have none of them in his pocket, tell him y'all don't have nothing to talk about until he does"

"Okay" I replied holding onto the money. Madam friend walked out first, and then she emerged out the room. "How did I do today Daddy?" She questioned with a big grin on her face.

"You did good, next time meet the quota, you made forty-seven hundred. Not bad, not bad at all. Let's go. We gonna' go out to eat somewhere nice tonight."

"You treat us so good" Madam said wrapping her arms around Big, she perked her lips preparing to kiss him. Big, pushed her back.

"Chill with that shit, you been sucking and fucking niggas all day. Keep yo' nasty lips off my face."

"I do this shit for you Motherfucka' don't

forget that," Madam hissed.

Big raised his hand and brought it down smacking her across the face sending her crashing into the floor. "Bitch, you better get some fucking act right, foe' I put my foot up ya' ass. Keep playing your ass gon' be back working the blade, with the rest of them bitches," Big roared a deranged look was on his face, something I had never saw before.

"Let's go baby girl," Big said walking out the door. I hurried behind him not wanting to get into trouble. I got to the door and looked back at Madam; she was pulling herself from the ground. I got to the car and my eyes lit up when I saw Kris sitting in the backseat.

"Are you okay?" he whispered. I shook my head up and down. Madam had finally made it to the car.

"Kris get up front, let Madam ride her ass in the fuckin' back."

Kris hopped into the front seat with Big, Madam was mad, you can tell, but she didn't utter a word to Big, just got into the car.

We didn't go out to eat' just went straight home to have Madam's fried bologna sandwiches.

Kris and I laid in bed trying to drown out the loud arguing coming from Big and Madam. I filled Kris in on my day with Madam; he did the same about his day with Big. The sounds only became louder. Kris and I closed our eyes hoping sleep would come to us before the loud sounds of Madam pleasing Big for her ill behavior took over.

Chapter 2

By the time I made it to 11, no longer was I talked to in riddles. Knowledge of the streets was given to me raw. I was no longer packed with a bag of toy's while out with Madam.

"You are old enough now Kandi, we not sugar coating shit anymore. When I was your age I already knew the deal and I am going to make sure you know the same. I'm going to teach you about this life. If you want to make it out of the ghetto, you gone have to learn some thangs to get you what you need."

"Like what?" I asked. She was speaking like I knew the life and what it consisted of.

"Using what you have, to get what you want. Your body is your temple and the most precious thing a women can have. I'm gon' show you how it's a money making enterprise too."

The taxi we were in pulled up to a rundown apartment complex, I never been to this one with Madam. Big couldn't bring us today, which is something that rarely ever happened. Big took Madam everywhere she needed to go.

Today was different, so we had to take a taxi; Madam wasn't too pleased with the taxi driver's service. We stepped out the taxi, and Madam, threw the money through the front window.

"Here, next time go the fuckin' way I tell you Motherfucka' you made me late." Madam said rudely.

"Let's go Kandi, made me fuckin' late" Madam was pissed, as she marched up the three flights of stairs.

"HURRY UP GIRL, WE ALREADY LATE AND YOU TAKING YOUR SWEET DAMN TIME," she yelled down the stairs at me. By the time I made it to the top of the stairs; I was out of breath.

"Time is money Kandi, and if you don't want to get your ass beat, you better hurry. These men pay for a certain time and they want it all."

Madam turned on her heels and marched up to a door, she knocked on it until a man opened it. His skin was ashy, his salt and pepper hair was balding, and his eyes were bright blue, instantly he gave me a bad vibe.

"Bitch, you were supposed to be here an hour ago, Big charges all that fuckin' money and you fuckin' late. You must gon' give me something extra for this inconvenience Choc." The girls in Big's stable were to call her Madam, but the streets and her tricks knew her ass of Choc.

"You know I got you sugar, Big needs to know nothing about this." Madam said, her voice had changed it was softer than before, it was more relaxed and calm. She walked into the apartment stroking the older man shoulders.

"Well get your ass in here and show me."

"C'mon Kandi," she said to me as she made her way deeper into the apartment.

"And who is this little lady? She here to help you?" The man asked, as we got deeper into the apartment, I could see it was two more men occupying the room, sitting on the tattered sofa.

"She is off limits," Madam said grabbing me closer to her. "She is here to watch and learn."

"Madam, I don't want to be here, I'm scared," I said to her. The three men eyes were fixed on me. They looked like hungry vultures that hadn't ate in days, and I was a juicy fresh piece of steak that they were ready to indulge in.

"Hush bitch, this is what you have to look forward to, this is the life; get fuckin' use to it. You just sit over there and watch me make this money. Make sure you learn something too," Madam said flinging me off of her. She quickly started to remove her clothes.

I wanted to run, but I didn't even know where I was. I stood frozen, I was scared and everyone eyes were on me, watching me. I closed my eyes hoping I would disappear, but it was to no avail I was still stuck there. No longer were their eyes on me. They were fixated on Madam, she was fully unclothed and her head was in between one of the men lap. Her head bobbed up and down on one man, while her hands pleased the other two. I was disgusted

19

with her, at them all. I found a corner; I pulled my knees to my chest and covered my ears trying to invade the loud sounds that escaped their mouths. The sounds only got louder and louder, they were far worst then the sounds she and Big made. I looked up and the position Madam was in with those men, I couldn't bare to be in the same room. I made a beeline to the door, running down the stairs until I couldn't hear them anymore. The few junkies standing around bickering now drowned out their moans. I took a seat at the bottom of the stairs and watched the people walk up and down the street never glancing my way.

I didn't know how long I had been out there watching the people fighting, the police arrived, and that didn't stop them. The sun had started to settle and now was replaced by the cool California breeze giving me a slight chill. I had been holding my pee since we arrived; I knew I wouldn't be able to go much longer without wetting myself. I refused to go back in there with Madam and her friends. The junkies kept walking pass me into a corner; I saw the small circle of junkies walk back pass out the door. I hurried towards the back of the staircase; it reeked of urine. I pulled down my pants and let the pee flow onto the concrete.

"You got a dollar?" I heard a voice ask. I looked around but didn't see anyone. It seemed like I was crying a river the way the urine continue to run down.

"Say, you gotta dollar?" I heard the voice

again, this time I could see the man slumped in the corner. I jumped getting pee on my pants.

"No," I said pulling my pants up and running back up to the first fight of stairs. I could hear the familiar sound of Big's Cadillac; I watched the entrance to the building hoping it was him. The cool breeze up against the pee on my pants made me even colder. I watched and watched and no Big, just as the tears wanted to fall from my eyes I heard my name.

"Kandi, what the fuck you doing out here?" I looked up to see Big at the bottom of the stairs.

"I couldn't sit in there with Madam, and her friends, doing those nasty things," I resorted looking up at him. I knew he wouldn't be too happy. I was ready for the beating I knew would come.

"How long have you been out here?"

"Since we got here, Big that's nasty what they are up there doing; I couldn't watch."

"Kandi, That's business, you gon' have to learn about this life. You are apart of the Timmons family, this is our life. So stop all that damn whining and scaring shit. You have to get prepared to take over the family enterprise."

"The life? Y'all keep yelling about this life, I don't want any parts of this. I don't want to be in this family then, I am not doing that nasty…." before I could finish my sentence Big's big hands landed across my face.

"Too fuckin' bad you are in this family, and you gon' do whatever I tell your black ass to do, understood?"

"Yes," I cried.

"Good, now go get your ass in the car, while I go get this bitch."

"I rushed down the stairs, hoping Kris was in the car. I made it to Big's Cadillac and Kris wasn't there. I could hear the screams; I looked up to find big dragging Madam to the car by her hair.

Madam got into the car and the dirty look she gave me, I knew her latest beating was due to me. Her vibe told me so. I just wanted to get home bathe and see my brother's face, but that didn't happen, we were out for hours. Big dropped Madam off where he dropped the other girls off. We sat in the car watching them, as they jumped in and out of cars and bringing Big money back every time.

"This is the life, in another year you will be ready Kandi, so make sure you pay attention and take notes, cause' when the time come; I don't want to hear all that cry baby bullshit that your black ass did today."

I just watched all of the women, letting Big's words fall on death ears.

Chapter 3

I remember the day like it was yesterday, when my brother and I turned 12. It's a day that I changed, I never looked at people the same from that day forward.

Big and Madam felt it was time for us to get out there and earn our stripes, bringing in our share to the family. '*Give the streets a taste of what would be the new generation of Bosses.*' They were tired of sugarcoating life for us. We were in the Embassy Suite, Hotel room 214, those numbers I will never forget. 'Hollywood is the city of the stars once you make it here, you made it to the big leagues.' Madam would always say. *"Only the Bad Bitches work in The Hollywood Hill's."*

Black Starr, was one of Big's bottom bitches, she was amongst the 20 other bitches in his stable. She walked into the room occupied by Kris, Big and I. Starr was 5 years older than me. But you couldn't tell from the low cut spandex red dress, 4 inch open toe clear pumps and blonde wig she sported, it looked horrible on her tar colored skin, the streets had aged the 17 year old way before her time.

"Starr honey, how are you?" asked Big.

"I'm good Daddy," Starr replied with a wide smile on her face. She had been down with Big, for the last three years, since her old pimp was murdered.

"Well today is the day I give my young protégé a taste of the empire that awaits him."

"Hey y'all," she spoke in her heavy southern accent. Starr was originally from the south, her mother moved to California to get away from her abusive husband, only to end up on drugs and exchanging her daughter for her next high. When the dealer wanted to keep Starr, she let him for a kilo of pure cocaine.

Kris and I just stood there and didn't utter a word, we were still naïve to what they really was expected of us. We had seen her around several times but we never engaged in conversation with her and hadn't planned on it. She wasn't liked by many and always gave me funny glares when Big and Madam weren't around.

"Don't y'all hear her speaking to y'all, show some fuckin' respect; I taught y'all ass better then that," Big roared.

"Hey," we responded dryly.

"They will be carrying on the Timmons family business, I need you to break my son in and show him some of your tricks. Take Kandi

down the hall with the Madam. I want you to
start with giving him some of that fire tongue
action and get his dick wet; he hung like his old
man," Big chuckled.

"C'mon Kandi" Starr said, walking out the
door. I slowly followed her down the hall. Starr
knocked on the door twice, and then opened it.
She walked in and I followed. Madam was
sitting on an older white mans lap, Mr. William
was his name. He was the old ashy guy from the
apartment complex; where we visited, I
remembered his perching blue eyes. I hadn't
seen him since that day, but I couldn't forget
those eyes.

"Madam, Kandi is here," Starr said leaving
me in the room with Madam and the old ashy
man.

Madam stood up and walked towards me she
glanced back over her shoulder "Sugar we will
be right back, enjoy another drink," Madam told
him. She grabbed a bag then she and I went into
the bathroom.

"Now listen Kandi, Mr. William, he is a
very dear friend of me and Big's, do you
remember him".

"Yeah, from the dirty apartment."

"Well he is going to be gentle with you,
and make you into a woman today; you
remember all the things I showed you when we
go on our business meetings? Well he paid very
good money for you today. So you show him a
good time, I'm going to be watching so don't
you dare be on any funny shit or Big will take

care of you. And we no you don't want that now do you?" Madam asked. Her face was stern, she could be the sweetest person one minute, and then flip like the drop of a dime at any given second.

She pulled items from the duffle bag she was carrying. She dressed me into a form fitting flora dress painted my face and applied shinny lipstick to my lips, She let my long shiny straight hair fall down my back and sprayed channel #5 on me, I remember the tears falling from my eyes, messing up the make-up she just had done.

"Stop fuckin' crying you messing up the damn make-up."

"I don't want to do this Madam, I don't want to go in there with him, I don't want to be a woman today," I cried.

"You betta' get yo' ass in there, and do anything that man ask of you. I have taken care of you since you came out my pussy bitch, get in there. It's time you make your own way and use what you got to take care of yourself. Now dry your fuckin' eyes before I give yo' black ass a reason to cry."

Madam waited until I dried my face, to fix the make-up. She opened the door and escorted me to the waiting Mr. William.

"Mr. William this is Kandi, Kandi this is Mr. William. Now sugar, you be gentle remember she is a virgin."

"Just the way I like them," Mr. William said with the biggest smile upon his face. If

26

looks could kill, he would have been dead, my
eyes would've torn him into shreds with the
stare I gave him, not wanting him to touch any
part of me, but it didn't faze him one bit. I
looked back at Madam and the same stern look
was on her face. I made my way closer to the
bed that Mr. William was sitting on. I looked
back again, over my shoulder at Madam. She
was now sitting in a chair, in the corner. She had
her left leg over her right and her arms folded
over her chest with her eyes fixed on me. Not
wanting to get beat by Big, which were the
worst. I made my way to the bed where Mr.
William was. He smiled as I got closer to him,
he reached his hand out to touch me and I
jumped.

"It's okay," he said. His bright blue eyes
piercing my skin, like an electric shot, I jumped
when he touched me. "You are so pretty, and
black."

I didn't say anything, because what I wanted to
tell him was to get his fuckin' hands off me.
That I wanted him to leave me alone, but knew I
would be beat once I got home. Mr. William
placed his hand on the strap of my dress and
pulled it down on both sides, until my dress hit
the floor exposing my young body. I had
nothing on and tears in my eyes, as he ran his
hand over my body, giving me the creeps. He
lifted my body off the ground and laid me on the
bed. He kissed my lips, then my neck and
shoulder. He made a trail down my body to the
center of my legs and buried his face in

between. I lay there silently crying out for help as he entered me taking away my innocence.

What lasted a few minutes, felt like a lifetime to me. When he was done handling his business he climbed off me, handed the money to Madam and departed.

I wasn't able to move, the pain I felt down there was unbearable, something I never felt before. I wanted to cry, but there was no longer a need or care to cry. I knew this was only the beginning, my life would forever be changed, and so did my attitude towards life.

"Why you still lying there?" Madam questioned when she was finished counting the money given to her.

I just looked at her, I was in pain but managed to pull myself up and slide back into the dress. I followed close behind her as we exited the room, and walked the short distance to the room where Big was.

She handed the money to Big, finally a big grin found its way onto her face. Big counted the crisp bills with a wide grin plastered on his face as well.

"Welcome to the team Baby girl, you gon' make the family a lot of money."

At that moment I wished I was bigger then him, I wanted to smack the grin from his face. I knew it was only a dream, Big was three times my size and his hands where bigger then my face. I took a seat and found refugee in my own personal thoughts. From that day forward my life had changed, hatred and anger plagued in my heart for Big and Madam.

That night when we got home, Big and Madam where ecstatic to know their young protégées were making their mark into the underworld of sex and carrying on the empire they built.

I lay wrapped in Kris's arms, the pain I was experiencing down below, was something I couldn't explain. I couldn't stop the bleeding; it ran right through the tissue I had lined in my underwear.

We could hear the music blasting, they were celebrating. On our way home they stopped and bought a bottle of the top shelf champagne for their celebration. They waited 12 long years for this moment. It was all business, never personal, even for the children they laid down and created. They always reminded us we were only an investment. The ten thousands dollars they made off my virginity, proved that fact.

No longer was I a child in their eyes. My breast began to develop, my hips began to spread and more of Madam's friends started to request for me.

While I rode with Madam, and witnessed the sexual acts she preformed with men and sometimes even women. Kris rode with Big, he was in training to take over and be the new pimp, pimping had changed since the days of the late Iceberg Slim. No longer were you able to pinpoint a pimp from his sharp dressing, fur coats or hand full of diamonds. They were replaced with gun toting gangstas' in foreign cars and sneakers. Big trained him to look for undercover police and other pimps, but mostly on how to instill fear into the working girls. If your women didn't respect you, didn't fear you, they weren't capable to bring your money back to you and jumping ship would come easy. If she disrespected you, you had to know how to discipline them accordingly to keep your clot in the streets. The worst thing is to be a pimp who didn't have his stable of bitches in line.

The months flew pass turning into years, I wasn't that innocent girl, like before I had changed. My heart no longer was pure; it had been plagued with hatred and animosity. With each passing day I began to become more and more adapted to the life of a hoe. No longer did I care or had the fight in me not to go. Kris on the other hand, didn't adapt to the life, he hated it.

On our 15th birthday, I woke up happy, I had been pinching money off the top of the money I had been earning while working the blade. I wanted to buy us something special for our birthdays. He had been acting strangely the last couple of weeks; I knew it was because he hated the life we were forced to live. I wanted to cheer him up, this was our life for now, and it didn't have to be our life forever. I repeated that to myself daily to cope with the fact, I grew to love sex.

I got up from my bed, walking over to his; I noticed it was empty and neatly made. I walked around the house calling his name; I got no answer but the echo of my own voice. Maybe he went with Big and Madam, I thought to myself. I was used to being left locked inside the house by myself.

I made my way back into the room I shared with Kris, to look for something to wear for the day. There was a paper sitting on my vanity mirror that I hadn't noticed before. I picked it up and instantly my heart sanked into my stomach.

"Kandi I can't take this anymore, I don't want this life for us, and we deserve more. I'm going to go out and make a better life for us, I'll do whatever I have to do, I just can't do this. I will comeback to get you, I promise."

Love your brother Kris.

I couldn't breathe, my knees buckled, I hit the ground. A river of tears cascaded down my face, I felt lost and betrayed. How could he leave me with them? The questions swarmed my mind. I cried, I cried until I couldn't cry anymore. My other half was gone, no longer was he by me. He left me by myself facing this horrible life. Who was going to care for me, love me, hold me while I cried about my sore feet or sore body.

When Big and Madam returned, they found me in that very same spot lost dried tears and snot on my face.

"Why the hell you on that damn ground? Get your ass up," Madam shouted walking pass; her words were just words without any meaning to me.

"Where is Kris? We have somewhere to be," Big asked.

I laid there, not answering them. I was lost "Where the fuck is Kris?" Big asked again. Still I didn't provide him with an answer. Using his foot, he lightly kicked me. "Answer me bitch" he yelled.

The letter was still crumbled in my hand. Madam leaned down and snatched it from my hand, I didn't fight her.

"Look at this shit, that little black nigga left," she hissed looking from me to Big.

"He left?" he asked quizzing. Snatching the paper from her hand. "How the fuck he do that?" Big asked. The house was locked from the outside, making us locked in when they weren't home, all the windows were locked as well

"She probably helped him," Madam sneered looking down at me.

They searched the house, Kris was in fact gone. They left back out without uttering a word to me.

Two days had past fast, I hadn't moved once. I was numb, but the stench that was coming from my body, I couldn't deal with any longer. Big and Madam had come and gone, never speaking a word to me, I knew they wouldn't allow me to lay there too much longer.

I got myself up and showered, the house was empty, and there wasn't a crumb of food anywhere in the house. I climbed into my bed, I sat there until I heard Big's car pull up. I dashed to the door, meeting them as they walked inside.

"So y'all just gone leave me in here with no fucking food," I yelled.

"You better calm your black ass down, before I fuck you up today," Madam said.

"Can I get some food?" I asked humbling myself, so that I could get some food, I hadn't eaten in days and was weak.

"Get her something to eat," Big said sitting down on the love seat in the living room.

"Why? She doesn't need shit, with that fucked up attitude, and the little stunt she pulled. Lying on that damn floor for days," Madam said as she straddled Big's lap.

"I didn't ask you, I told you, now do what the fuck I said, shit yo' ass always got some fuckin' back talk. Do what the fuck I tell you," Big said pushing her off his lap.

Madam got up and made her way into the kitchen to make me a plate of the Louisiana's they brought in with them. Pissed she had to make me a plate she dropped the plate on the floor in front of me.

"Eat up little bitch."

"I can't stand you," I said to her. It was the truth; I hated everything about her. I hated the way she talked, walked and how she looked.

Madam laughed "good bitch."

"Both of you bitch's shut the fuck up," Big yelled.

I was getting to a breaking point everyday it was something new, I knew I couldn't run I didn't have anywhere to go. I contemplated killing myself; Hell couldn't have been any worst then the life I was living, it felt like hell on earth anyway.

"That dress to fucking little, take it off now," Madam said looking me from my head to my toes.

"Nah its cool, nobody here" Big said, licking his lips. "That's a good little outfit for the blade, you had enough rest make sure your ass ready to get back out there and make that money tomorrow."

"Take your ugly ass in your room" Madam said, she hated the way Big looked at me. I didn't care, I was better off sitting in my room looking at all the dirty pale walls then them anyway. I marched my way into my room, making sure to put an extra hump into my walk, because I knew they were watching.

"Don't try to be slick bitch, I'm watching you," Madam said.

With each passing day and trick I turned, my body started to fill out and the natural sway of my hips hypnotized every man in passing including Big. Madam knew he wanted me, she wasn't sure if he had already had some. She wouldn't go anywhere that would be leaving me and him alone, but as much as she tired, Big kept her busy.

Chapter 4

Big and Madam had been gone most of the day, leaving me locked in the house like always. Dark started to fall, I knew Big would be home any minute; I hadn't been to work since Kris left. I knew he was going to see to it that I made every penny he lost, because I was out. In this life it was a twenty-four hour, seven days a week hustle, three hundred and sixty-five days. There wasn't any 401k plan, paid sick days. While I was hurting, he was losing money, and that wasn't tolerated.

Big walked into the house, I noticed Madam wasn't behind him.

"I'm almost ready," I said to him.

"It's cool," he replied standing in the entrance of my room watching me. I knew what time it was, Madam wasn't home and he was ready for some. I could feel his eyes watching me, I looked his way and the look in his eyes showed me what I already knew. He was horny and my night started now, him being my first trick, and repayment for his lost wages.

"You know you cost me a lot of money when you had your little fit because your punk ass brother left? You better go out there tonight and serve them tricks right, and get my money. You can warm up and start with giving me some of that wet shit, the way I like," Big said backing me against the bed.

Big dropped his pants and his erect penis was sticking up. He had a no panty rule on the blade, so he knew I didn't have any on. I pushed my skirt up, letting him find his way inside of me.

We had been going at it for over an hour, Big was aging but his stamina was out of the roof. I heard a car pull into the driveway, I knew it had to be Madam; no one else was to come to our home. When I heard the struggle with the keys, due to the deadbolts on the door. I knew it was Madam; a slight grin graced my face. I winded my hips harder, riding Big even faster then ever. He was so occupied at how his dick plunged in and out of me to hear the door open and close. I could hear light foot steps in the long hallway leading to my room from the entrance of the house. I went into full actress mode, bouncing up and down, *"Fuck me harder, yeah. Yeah Daddy"* I cried out.

My bedroom door slowly opened. I looked back, our eyes connected and I smiled harder then I ever did in life. There it was, in front of her, a sight I knew she despised more then anything. Her husband taking a deep dip into my overflowing chocolate fountain. She was vexed; she dropped the bags in her hand. She charged full force to the bed, viciously pulling me off of Big by my hair.

"You dirty bitch!" Madam roared striking my body, with an open hand. I tried to fight her off, but she had a better advantage. I swung wildly, forcing her to back up a tad bit. I made a beeline to the door, she rushed behind me. Big was so confused on what was going on, he was still laid up in my bed. Madam grabbed the broomstick charging me, swinging it wildly.

"C'mon on bitch! You wanted to fuck my man like you grown, come get this ass whooping then." Madam was determined to beat my ass; I was determined to fight my best fight with her. I was backed into the corner, she continually whacked me with the broom, and I took every hit. I knew she would grow tired, that's when I would attack. Just as I predicted, Madam moved slower she had grew tired. I leaped like a spider, wrapping my legs around her body, she couldn't move. Using a close fist, I pounded on her face, head and anywhere else I could.

"WHAT THE FUCK IS GOING ON?" Big yelled finally coming after us. There he stood with no pants and his boxers dangling around his ankles. He separated us, standing in between us, he looked from me to Madam; looking for an answer.

"GET THIS BITCH OUT OF HERE, NOW!" Madam shouted a look of disgust on her face.

I knew I was enticing the situation with the smirk on my face; Madam lunged across Big's husky frame.

"Get the fuck out of my house, you nasty tramp" she ranted.

"Calm the fuck down, this my shit, I make the fuckin' rules." Big, said pulling up his boxers.

"So you think it's cute to fuck this little dirty tramp, in my house?" Madam asked, she was begging for a beating questioning Big.

"Bitch, don't forget who the fuck I am, I run this shit. What the fuck you thought, I wasn't fuckin' that." He pointed to me. "You know I've fucked half of the girls. So why the fuck you acting silly tonight?"

"Paul Timmons," Madam had tears cascading down her face, I never heard her call Big, by his government name. "If that ugly tramp doesn't leave this house tonight, neither you nor she will be alive come morning. Remember why you keep me around, I know everything. Get her out of here." Madam said calmly, it was the strange psychotic look on her face, which sent a slight fear in me. Her face showed the hatred she had for me.

Big turned and faced me, "pack your shit and bounce Kandi." He stormed out the living room, knocking over the lamp.

"Let the bitch go find her punk ass brother."

"I'm cool with that, if I knew this is all it would take to get the fuck away from y'all, I would have been let you catch us. Don't be mad, my pussy tighter and wetter," I said dashing to my room to pack a small bag. I went back into the living room, Madam sat on the recliner smoking a blunt.

"Don't let me ever catch you around my man again, bitch."

"Your man, ha funny" I said laughing. "Big is a fuckin' pimp bitch. You're his hoe, why he chose to marry you baffles me. You are the same as me, and every other bitch in his stable, a fuckin' price tag."

"GET THE FUCK OUT" she yelled. Jumping from her seat, the door had already been unlocked. I stood there looking at her; I knew it got under her skin.

"I said get the fuck out bitch" she pushed me out the door, sending me flying to the ground, face first.

Madam had been on the streets since she was 12 years old. Her mother was dead, killed by the hands of her abusive boyfriend. She never knew her father or knew any family members to turn to. She was placed in foster care, where she got introduced to drugs and sex at a young age. By the age of 14, she had met Big, then age 32 and fell into his rapture of Pimpin'. By the age of 16 she was giving birth to Kris and me. Her once curvy body didn't snap back just as she would have liked. There were no more succulent boobs or washboard stomach they were replaced with saggy boobs and a small gut. I was the spitting image of what she used to be in her prime, and that posed a threat to her, and she hated me for it.

With a small bag in hand, I got up off the ground and dusted myself off. I was more then happy to get as far away from them as I could, even if that meant I would be homeless. With nowhere else to go I hit the blade, it was like a home to me anyway. I spent so much time there; I knew this wasn't an end. Big and Madam were known on the streets, my days there wouldn't last long, Big had major pull with the police, tricks and other working girls.

Chapter 5

I remember the icy cold winter air hitting my face. It was mid-November and twelve at night. I clinched the thin jacket around me as I walked swiftly down Broadway, towards the Blade.

"You need a ride youngin?" It was a dude in a dark blue truck with tinted windows. With the window half way down, all I could see was the New York Yankees fitted cap he wore and his eyes.

"Nah, I'm good …thanks anyway," I replied. I was young, but not green to the streets Big made sure of that.

I continued to walk down the street. There wasn't any buses running and without two pennies to my name a cab was out the question. It took me 45 minutes to get to the blade. I made it to Figueroa, known to many as Fig, one of the major streets for Prostitution. The block was live; I continued my stride down Fig until I made it to 120th shopping center. There were a lot of working girls out, most I knew. I walked up to a small crowd of girls, a few I knew some I hadn't seen. That was normal, new girls' always surface day in and out. Ecstasy, Bambi, and Peaches were standing watching the heavy flow of traffic looking for their next date.

"Hey Kandiland, where you been? And what you doing out so late? Where Daddy Big at?" Ecstasy asked looking around for Big; she was one of his hoes."

"I don't have anywhere else to go, that black bitch put me out."

"Who?" Bam asked.

" Madam?" Peaches quickly asked looking around for the duo.

"Yeah" I said to them, I could see the girls were kind of nervous, they kept looking around waiting for Big to show up.

"What Big say about this?"

"He told her no, and then she said she would kill us, if I stayed there, so he told me to get my shit and leave."

"Damn that's fucked up, you need anything?"

"Nah, I'm good Bam, thanks anyway. I'm about to go in here to change and try to make me some money"

"Okay when Big come to collect, you want me to tell him you out here? He may take you to the spot," Ecstasy asked, I knew her loyalty was with Big.

"Nah fuck him, and that bitch. I'm good, I'm out here on a solo money making mission."

"Okay, well we haven't seen you!" Bam said checking her surroundings.

"Nope," said Peaches.

"You know we got you, it has been live out here, go change so you can make you some ends to get some food and a room," Ecstasy said.

"Okay, thanks y'all" I told the girls as I made my way towards the McDonalds to change.

"Aye Kandi," Bam called out to me. I turned around to face her.

"Be careful, you know this is a dangerous game to be out here with no back up."

"I will," I said giving her a half smile. I knew I was playing with fire, but I didn't see any other options, it was all I knew.

Ecstasy, Bambi and Peaches were all in Big's stable, but they always looked out for me since I was the youngest. They had been on the streets a long time and had seen it all.

Within two hours I had made 300 dollars, I was tired with everything that took place I was ready to shower and get some rest. I went to grab my bag from the side of the trash bin when I saw the same blue truck pull up.

"What's good youngin'? I see you bout yo' shit, but I can upgrade you, you too pretty to be out here pounding the pavement."

"I don't know what you talking about Sir, but you have a good night."

I wasn't dumb, I knew he figured out I was a hoe, he was trying crack me and take me home to get down with him.

"I been watching you lil' momma, I seen you jump in and out about five cars, so I know you working"

I didn't say anything. I scanned the streets looking for any familiar faces, but saw none. The police had gotten hot, so it cleared out. *"Fuck"* I said to myself. I lingered around the parking area, so did the truck, he kept circling the parking lot. When I noticed the car hadn't come back around in 10 minutes, I started to head down Fig, trying to hurry and make the short distance to the Spot. The Spot was a little shady motel that a lot of working girls used to turn tricks, the owner was a real pervert and loved getting his dick sucked. So I knew he wouldn't have a problem giving me a room for the night.

I was a few blocks away from the Spot when I heard a car stop behind me, I continued to walk picking up my pace never looking behind me. I heard the car door shut and footsteps behind me. I had a feeling something didn't feel right. I didn't look back, I just gripped my bag and made a run for it, but I wasn't fast enough as my attackers where right on me.

One tripped me making me loose my balance falling to the ground. I started to swing my hands wildly trying to get away, but the tight hold one had on my waist and hands were unbreakable. I started to scream to the top of my lungs. "HELP! HELP! HELP ME!" I screamed helplessly hoping someone would hear me, see me, and rescue me.

"Shut the fuck up bitch," it was the dude that was wearing the Yankees cap in the truck, I recognized his voice.

"FUCK YOU," I screamed.

Not expecting it, he delivered a blow to my face, busting my nose and lip on impact.

"Bitch I said shut the fuck up. You could have made it easy for your self, but you wanted to be a little stuck up bitch. So this what you get, put this bitch in the car maybe then she will shut the fuck up. We about to have fun with her ass, tonight."

They hadn't paid much attention to their surroundings, or they would have seen the car on the opposite corner of the street with its light out. I prayed the occupants would help me.

I closed my eyes, hoping this wasn't the way my life would end. I saw feet moving towards us.

"What the fuck going on here?" It was the three occupants from the car who watched the whole ordeal go down. They were armed with 3 semi automatic handguns pointed at the Yankees cap man and his friends.

"Yo my dude, y'all need to mind y'all business, and let me handle mine, y'all don't got shit to do with this Cuh'" it was Yankees cap talking.

"You okay?" The dude asked not worrying about what Yankees cap was saying.

Yankees cap hawked at me, threating me with his eyes not to speak. "Nah I'm not, these muthafuckas' tryna kidnap me, I don't even know these niggas," I said. It was my only way to try and escape. The daggers Yankees cap shot at me were deadly.

"Check this out Blood, I'm going to give you an option. We can handle this on some G shit, but we see you niggas' not built for that, because y'all not even strapped and kidnapping a fuckin' girl. So just let the girl go or my niggas gone blow your brains all over this concrete."

The dude who had me pent up looked at Yankees cap for reassurance.

"Let the bitch go, she not even worth it. But I will see you again little bitch without these niggas." Yankees cap said, backing up towards his car.

"You should watch your choice of words Blood," The guy spoke. I was pushed to the ground as shots rang off killing Yankees cap and his two friends. I felt a pair of strong arms pick me up from the ground, and then put me into a car.

"Yo'! What's your name?"

"Kandi"

"Well Kandi I'm Ice, these my homies, Yoda and Duce."

"Thank you guys for helping me, I don't know what they would have done to me if y'all didn't rescue me."

"It's cool, can we drop you off somewhere?"

"Yeah," I ran off the directions to the Spot. I sat back as they blasted the music and passed around a blunt making small talk, which I couldn't understand.

"You smoke Kandi?"

"No" I said, even thought the sweet aroma of the weed was intoxicating to my nostrils.
It didn't take us much time to reach the Spot, the car slowed down then stopped in front of the Spot.

"Umm Sweetie, you sure this where you going? This a known place…"

"For hoes," I said cutting him off. He looked at me from the rear view mirror."Yeah I'm a hoe, what do you have to say about it?"

"Was ole dude your Pimp or what y'all call them you're Daddy?" Ice asked glaring at me.

"Nah, my parents are my pimps, they just put me out. I have no where else to go, but here." I said my eye's never leaving his. I knew what life I was in, so why be scared to admit it, this was life, and his opinion about my life didn't matter.

"I'm sorry, but I wouldn't feel comfortable leaving you here after what happened tonight. I have a place, I'm not there much, and you can stay there until you figure something out."

Without even letting me object, he pulled off. Turning the music back up and continued the conversation with his friends.

"What a night, get kicked out, almost kidnaped and now in the car with three dudes who saved my life. But I don't know shit about them." I said praying they were on the up and

up.

The ride wasn't too far, when the car stopped I looked out the window and was surprised by my surroundings. I was born on the gritty streets of LA, and spent most of my days on the blade. Standing in front of something like this wasn't my norm, I could get used to living like this. I thought to myself as I looked around at the waterfront apartment complex and I couldn't believe this was true. The cool breeze from the beach felt nice against my bruised skin.

Ice opened the door. "We here Kandi, c'mon. Yoda, Duce come get me in the morning bright and early." He said to his friends grabbing my bag. We entered the large glass door and got on the elevator, he pushed the 25th floor.

When we walked through his door, I was speechless again at the spacious and immaculate dwellings. His apartment was one I saw in the magazines, something I had never stepped foot in and couldn't believe I was now.

"Here is a shirt and some boxers, there's towels in the bathroom cabinet. You can get cleaned up and here is some medicine, I know your head has to be hurting. Make yourself comfortable. I will be in the living room, if you need anything. The remote is on the night stand."

"Thank you! Thank you for saving my life, I don't know what they would have done to me. And thanks for letting me stay the night."

"It ain't nothing Sweetie, have a good night's rest."

I showered and laid in the bed. It was so big and soft, it was so different then the small hard bed I normally slept on. I drifted off to sleep fast. I woke up the next morning, Ice was gone. He left a note and some money on the kitchen table.

"I had to split, but here is some money, buy you some clothes. You can stay as long as you need to."

I didn't know where I was, I put on some clothes I had in my bag. I took a twenty from the stack of money Ice left and grabbed the key card. I went out the same way we came in last night. The streets in front of the complex was filled with people, lots of white people walking dogs, running and riding bikes. I wrote the numbers down from the building on the small pad, I took from Ice's apartment. I found the street name and jotted it down. I walked until I found a pay phone and called a taxi. As I waited for the taxi, I watched the people walking pass, some looked my way some didn't. It was so different then the streets I was use to seeing. The taxi pulled up, I jumped in and gave them the streets to the blade.

It was late when I got back to Ice's apartment, he wasn't home and it didn't appear that he had been. I showered and fell asleep as soon as my head hit the pillow.

Pounding The Pavement

Chapter 6

Over the next few weeks, Ice and I had became more acquainted with each other and shared our life stories. For the first few nights, I went and hit the blade while Ice was out. I wanted to have my own money, I didn't want to become a financial burden on him, housing and feeding me, he even was clothing me because I didn't have anything; but I wanted my own. I was too used to always having to depend on someone to handle my needs. Ice didn't mind and quickly put an end to me hitting the blade. I got home, one night and Ice was waiting for me.

"Kandi, if you gon' stay here, you need to quit that shit."

"What you talking about Ice?" I knew what he was talking about.

"Kandi, I understand that lifestyle is all you know. But, I can't sit here and allow you to do that from my home. So either you go enroll in school or something, so you can stay here or hit the streets the choice is yours."

"Thanks, I never been to a regular school. I

was home schooled, can you help me?"

"Sure, when I get back into town."

"Thanks again for all your help."

"It's cool."

The first few weeks were different for me, the blade was all I knew, but I couldn't lie, I liked the change. I grew to love and sometimes even craved sex, I was accustomed to fucking five or more men a night. To let my body rest, and not hear demands of men requesting sexual favors from me was new, but I loved it.

Ice was an upcoming rapper born and raised on the streets of Compton. He was well known throughout Compton and the surrounding cities for his quick gritty punch lines.

From the night he saved my life he promised he would take care of me, and that he did. He said he wanted to give me a better life than I had in my past, being young and naive I believed him. He did everything he had said he would, so why wouldn't I believe him.

I remember the night of his highly anticipated Mix Tape release party. We had been out shopping on Melrose all day. He showered me with gifts, name brands I couldn't even pronounce. I was in school and had scored a perfect 100 on my first test. His way of showing me how proud he was that I was able to turn my life around, was a shopping spree. Being young and not used to that, I felt on top of the world.

"Keep up the good work Kandi, and you will see more of this. Go upstairs and get ready, the car will be here soon."

"Thank you Ice," I said making my way upstairs for a quick shower then to get dressed. I didn't know if Ice was attracted to me, or he was just truly a gentleman. It had been 2 months since he saved my life, and never once, had he made a pass at me. I wasn't used to that, I was used to men throwing themselves at me. But he never gave that impression that sex was something he wanted from me. I thought maybe it was because he knew my past, that I once was paid to have sex. I knew many men would never make a hoe their woman, it was like taboo.

I retreated upstairs to the master bedroom and quickly picked out the form fitting knee length black dress, we got earlier. I always heard a woman should own at least one little black dress. I slid the dress onto my skin, it fit perfect. It hugged every curve of my body. I slid the lip gloss, Glass by Mac over my lips, it felt so different then the lip gloss I stole from the beauty salon. I slid into the strappy black heels. I admired myself in the mirror, it wasn't the first time I saw myself in this attire, I was born a hoe, and this was my normal attire for a nights work. The fabric felt better and looked better on my skin. It wasn't the cheap spandex material like I normally got from the local swap meets; the price tag said it was priced at 285.00 dollars.

I stood admiring myself in the mirror for what felt like hours, I was pleased with the person I was looking at in the mirror.

"Kandi?" Ice called out from behind me.

"Hey, is it time to go?"

"Yeah, and you look beautiful" he smiled. Showing off the dimple in his chin.

"Thank you," I replied. I had never been called beautiful.

"Come on, the car is out front."

The elevator ride was filled with Ice on the phone talking business in codes. I knew Ice was much more then a rapper, his demeanor gave that impression. We walked the short distance to an all white on white Porsche truck; we climbed into the butter cream seat, and the driver pulled off. Ice remained on the phone the whole ride until we pulled up to a venue in Hollywood.

The driver opened the door, the outside was packed. Ice stepped out first then he helped me out. The bright lights flashed from the cameras and the people outside screamed Ice name. I knew it was all about him, but it made me feel special, like I was someone.

We were led to the VIP area bottles of liquor were waiting at the tables, women stood around in the skimpiest outfits waiting for him to arrive. When the DJ announced his arrival the crowd went ballistic.

I sat back and enjoyed a drink, as I watched him entertain his fans. When he hit the stage he commanded everyone's attention as he spitted his lyrics to his latest tune '*Hub City Finest*' and moved around the stage captivating everyone's attention with his quick rhymes over the smooth beat. I couldn't help but move to the smooth beat as his lyrics glided over it in the crowded club.

Ice was 5'7 with honey brown colored skin, he was medium built and well-toned. He was dressed in some crispy Levi's and a Compton hoodie; He rocked an Iced out Jesus Piece with matching black diamonds. He delivered punch line after punch line about his life in Compton. I hadn't realized my eyes were closed, until I heard my name being called. I thought I was hearing things until I made eye contact with Ice, and he called my name again.

"Kandi come up here," Ice yelled over the Mic. I was escorted to the stage where Ice and his crew stood.

"This here my little mama, Kandi. When y'all see her in the streets, show her respect and know that this me," Ice said to the crowd. I was taken back by his words. He leaned in and gave me a wet kiss. I was confused by his actions but didn't want to make him look bad so I kissed him back. The crowd went insane by the scene. The music blared back up and Ice ripped song after song. I stayed on the stage and moved to the beat until he finished his set. We were escorted off the stage and into a small room.

"What was that about Ice?" I asked once we were alone.

"Kandi, I know about your past and over the few months I have watched you convert into a young woman, and I want you for myself." I was stunned by his words he hadn't shown any interest in me, I had been with tons of men in my short life. Ice didn't give me any signs he wanted me.

"You want me for yourself? Like what?"

"As my woman, the only nigga you give that pussy to," he said.

"Wow, I didn't even think you liked me in that way, you never showed me any attention in that way."

"I didn't want you to feel like that was all I wanted. I know you come from a past, that all men saw you for was sex. I know people have hurt you in the past, I'm not trying to be that person. I wanted to give you time to handle you, but I can't wait no longer little mama, I gotta have you."

How could I tell this man no, he had saved my life, took care of me. I wasn't sure what he expected of me, I knew nothing about being someone's woman. I was only 15 years old, life had been delivered to me like I was grown. But I was still a young teen, who never had a boyfriend, tricks were the only thing I knew outside of Big.

"Yes, yes Ice, I will be your woman," I said to him. I appeared excited, but deep down I was scared. I didn't know if I could be what he wanted.

Ice took me into his strong arms, tightly embracing me. Our lips locked doing a dance to its own beat. He carried me to a love sofa in the room and sat me on his lap. He rose my dress to my waist and let his fingers collide with my wet vagina as he moved in and out slowly. I tugged at his waist until I had his pants unbuckled; I stroked his thick manhood until he was rocked hard. I slid my thong off and straddled him, I took it slow I hadn't had penetration in so long. Once I had him in fully I slowly grinded my hips against his until we were fuckin' each other, his strong hands guided me up and down his long thick man hood. We sexed each other on the sofa until we both erupted in natural bliss. It was the first time I could actually say I enjoyed sex, it felt different with Ice than I had ever experienced. I felt a connection with him, like he was trying to learn my body and please it to my satisfaction. When we finished we didn't utter a word we fixed ourselves and made our way back into the club and partied the night away.

When we got home that night we sexed each other until the rise of the sun and formed a wicked kind of love for each other.

From then it was constant partying, Ice was becoming a household name. From doing shows and hosting parties, partying had become our life. Drinking and drugs also came with the partying. When I wasn't trying to get caught up in school I was sleep recovering from a hang over and preparing for the next one. We were living life in the fast lane, we had enough money to do what we wanted and Ice did everything he wanted. Money was never his problem, when we were low he made a few calls and more money was brought to us.

Life was good, I was living in a dream. The money flowed like water out of a faucet. But just like anything that comes easy, it disappears just as easy. Ice had quickly made a name for himself and with that came haters, so-called friends and family all wearing a disguise. Ice had become lost in his new fame and grew to be arrogant. He felt money wasn't anything he had tons more, when we went out he splurged on everyone handling ever thing. *"If I got it, my niggas got it, all my niggas gone eat with me."*

Yeah I was enjoying the life Ice provided for me, it was different. But the constant partying, drinking and smoking was taking a toll on my body. I couldn't eat unless I was high, I had to have a drink everyday. It seemed like I left my old life to find another one that wasn't too much better. Yeah I didn't have to sell my body every night to dudes, just one Ice. I was paying for the shopping sprees, he wanted sex on demand. At first I didn't mind, he was my man, it was my duty to please him. But he was turning into someone I didn't know anymore, wanting sex in places filled of people. He was popping more pills then a person with a chronic illness. He was usually too messed up to make it to the studio. Less and less they started to see him, he began to not show up at appearances at the clubs and shows.

When he realized money wasn't flowing like it had been before and my constant nagging he finally made his way back into the studio to release some new material he had inside of him. But it was too late, he found out those who once believed in him had lost their faith. After taking a lot of grief because of his slacking and mistakes his manger let him go. Clubs didn't want him to host their parties anymore, he was losing everything he worked so hard for. The people who were there when the money was, slowly disappeared. When Ice realized he was only a benefit to people, now he was down no one was around, he became angrier. People he loaned money to couldn't be found. His growing addiction began to increase as he stressed making him even angrier. His life wasn't how he planned it, he worked hard and it all seemed to go down the drain. With the increase of drugs I noticed a change in him, he became verbally abusive towards me, the only person left in his corner.

"I was doing good until I started fucking with you, spending my money on making you look good. You fucked my homies hunh? That's why they stopped fucking with me. They told me not to try and wife up no hoe, hoes not meant to be wives. Hell not even girlfriends, just fucks."

"I never asked you for shit Ice."

"And you never turned shit down either."

"I have always showed my appreciation for everything you have did, and bought for me Ice. Your friends stop fucking with you, because they were never your real friends. And was mad because I wasn't fucking them, they all offered to fuck me behind your back, I politely declined."

"Yeah whatever, that's what you say" Ice said leaving out the door. That had become his new thing when he didn't have an answer or when I didn't do as he said.

I grabbed my backpack and left the house, I had been slacking in school, and I was going to meet up with my study group to prep for a test.

It was after 10pm when I got home, the condo was dark and I didn't see Ice car outside. I threw my bags down in the living room, and dashed to the bathroom. I had been holding my pee for the last hour, on the train ride home. The bathroom was dark only illuminated with the night light. I turned on the light and I jumped at the figure sitting in the empty bathtub. It was Ice, he sat in the empty bathtub shooting up.

"What the fuck are you doing Ice?"

"Bitch close the fucking door and get the fuck out."

"Ice, you better then this just put it down," I pleaded with him.

"What do you know about being better then something, you're a hoe now get the fuck out before I make you suck my dick while I get high."

I rushed out the bathroom back into the living room. I couldn't believe my eyes, Ice never talked about his immediate family. I didn't know whom to call to help him, I knew he was spiraling out of control and death was on his back. I wanted to leave but I didn't have anywhere to go. I didn't want go back to the streets. I didn't want to look backwards only forward. After 3 hours Ice finally emerged from the bathroom. He didn't say anything just left out the door. I watched him, from the patio, he staggered down the street. I didn't see his car anywhere, at that time I didn't know how bad his drug addiction was, he had sold his car in exchange for drugs.

I tried to sleep that night but I couldn't. I tossed all night, there was so much on my mind. The only peace I had in my life was slowly vanishing once again, I was empty and lost. I often came home to find items in the house missing, it was his stuff, so I never put up much of an argument.

It was my 16th birthday I came home after celebrating with some of my classmates, he wasn't home enough to remember. I didn't dare remind him, he was so angry and bitter. I walked into the apartment to find him packing a bag of stuff he bought me.

"What's going on Ice? How are you feeling today?" I asked, I didn't know his mental space.

"Where your ass been at Kandi? You out there, giving my pussy away already? Cause' a nigga down and out."

"Ice you fuckin' trippin', did you forget it's my birthday, I went out with some friends from school."

"You don't have no fuckin' friends, don't play with me Kandi, you out here fucking someone else, huh? Just tell me the real, I know your kind."

"My kind? Those drugs got you all fucked up Ice, where are you going with my stuff?"

"Didn't my money pay for this shit?"

I didn't give him an answer, he knew his money

paid for it.

"That's what the fuck I thought."

I just watched him pack my things shoes, purses and clothes.

"Give me some money and you can keep your stuff," Ice said.

"How am I supposed to give you money Ice? I don't have any money and you know that shit.

"You know how to get some, I got some niggas lined up."

"You expect me to fuck your so called friends to support your drug habit? That shit you smoking really fuckin' your head up."

"Bitch it's not something you haven't done before. Don't forget where you came from, because you can easily find your ass back there."

I couldn't believe my ears, here this crack head was throwing up my past in my face, like his shit was better. I thought to myself.

"Well since you don't have no money for me and not trying to go out and make any, I'm out" Ice said gripping the bag and headed for the door.

I watched Ice walk out the door, I knew our time was wearing out. He wasn't the ambitious man I met so many months ago. I showered and climbed into the bed. It smelled like the old Ice, the memories that we shared in that very same bed flooded my vision as the tears streamed down my face. Yet again another person used me, used me all up until I served no purpose to him. I cried myself to sleep.

It was way into the wee hours, I heard movement in the house. I thought it was Ice looking for something else in the house to steal and trade for drugs. I didn't get out of bed, until I heard the footsteps get closer to the room and I noticed it was more than one set. I sat up, and was met with a screwed off shotgun pointed at my head.

"Who the fuck are you?" I asked.

"Shut the fuck up and follow my directions, simple and easy. If not I can turn that white wall behind your head crimson, the choice is yours." The man said, his deep voice scared me.

"I don't have anything," I said to them hoping they believed me, I was terrified and didn't want my life to end, even as shity as it was.

"I didn't tell your ass to speak," the man said hitting me with the gun. "Where is the fuckin' money?"

"I don't have any money," I said in agony from the blow I sustained.

"Ice said you had the 400.00 dollars he owe us, and we want our money, right now!"

"He lied, I don't have any money, and you can take whatever is left in this house. It all belongs to him, but I don't have any money to give you."

The man swung the gun multiply times against my face. "You lying to me bitch?" he yelled.

"No" I cried out.

"Tie this bitch up, Ice said we can get some pussy, if she didn't give up the money."

I tried to fight, but they overpowered me. They

were too strong.

They tied me up, ripped my clothes off and for hours they each took turns raping me. They laughed and joked as they pounded away inside of me. They kept pounding until they felt their debt from Ice was paid in full. Never in my whole life had I felt more violated as I laid in bed my body numb and sore from the hours of torture and all the ejaculation that was all over my body. I was humiliated, I felt life slipping from me. I had to get away, this was slowly killing me and I felt suicide consuming me again. This was far worst then my first sexual experience.

I couldn't move I laid in the very same spot where hours ago I was being raped. I heard the door open. I jumped, scared that it was them coming back for round two. But it was Ice.

"Damn what the fuck happened to you?" He laughed standing in the bedrooms door snacking on a bag of chips. His once radiant honey brown skin was now dry and dirty looking; ashy lips the drugs were eating him alive. He no longer was the man, I had fallen head over hills for, and he was neither gentle nor kind anymore. I looked at him, I didn't say anything.

"Looks like you been fuckin' in my house? You must have some money for me, then?" With every fiber in my body I wanted to get up and beat him to a bloody pulp. How could he find this funny when my anal was still bleeding from the constant ramming of three different size penises having their way with it?

"Three men came here tonight, looking for you. They said you owed them money and they wanted it tonight."

"Okay so did you give it to them shit?"

"I don't have no fuckin' money Ice, you know that. They fuckin' raped me; all three of them."

He just looked at me, his face held no expression.

"Don't act like you never fucked three niggas at once, oh only if the price right huh? That's what you hoe's be saying. That's a woman's job to handle her man's affairs and business." He walked out the room never asking me if I was okay.

"Oh Kandi," he shouted back. "Good job babe, now I can go cop from someone else with that money you saved me." He laughed locking his self in the bathroom.

I couldn't stop the tears that poured from my eyes. This man said he loved me that he would take care of me, not do what Big did to me. But in my eyes, Ice was far worst, he promised me, he would take care of me, only for him to leave me, raped and beaten.

Chapter 7

Every day it was something new and the emotional toll it was putting on me was too much, I was at a breaking point but I didn't have anywhere to go. My thoughts went to my brother, I hadn't seen him since the day he left.

It was a Friday night and Ice wasn't home like always. I sat in the living room going through the pile of mail of all the bills that were in delinquent and threatened to be cut off. The rent hadn't been paid in two months the manger wanted us out. It had been a long time since I hit the blade, I knew I would have to, in order to bring some money into the house or we would be assed out. I loved the apartment and how it sat over the water and showed the mountains in the distance. I knew life was about to deal me a few more bad cards. I would have to be on the blade, day in and day out to get the money for this life style. I knew I could get the money, I knew it was sad to admit, but I was good at what I did.

I cleaned what was left in the condo and then ran me a nice hot bath and soaked in the Jacuzzi tub my mind was everywhere, there was so much to think about. I soaked for hours, until my skin was wrinkled and the water was ice cold. I went to the local clinic and had a sexual transmitted disease and aids screening. After the ordeal, I didn't know what I could have caught. Big and Madam always instilled in their girls, regular check-ups.

I took some Motrin, for the slight headache I had. I got into bed and was off to sleep as soon as my head hit the pillow.

I awoke to the bed moving, I heard voices. I thought I was dreaming. But the bed wouldn't stop shaking.

"Yeah… yeah daddy, fuck this pink pussy," the woman moaned. I turned over and got the shock of my life. Ice was fucking another chick right next to me.

I couldn't believe my damn eyes I was furious how dare he. I saw red as I yelled and lunged toward the woman. "You nasty white bitch," I said throwing punches at her. "You come into my home and fuck my man in my bed next to me, how fucking nasty are you," I couldn't stop I was fed up. I took my anger for Ice on his snow bunny.

"Kandi," Ice called out. "Let her go shit," he laughed still laying in the bed watching the ordeal. "C'mon babe let the bitch go, your ass crazy," Ice said. I looked at him ready to attack his ass next.

"I'm sorry I didn't know you were home," the girl cried. I didn't care I was too pissed to see straight I started to see blood pour from her face. I let her go "Get the fuck out my house bitch and don't you ever come back here." The girl grabbed her stuff without even putting her clothes on and rushed out the door never looking back.

"Your ass crazy, why you beat the bitch up? I needed some fuckin' pussy shit."

"You're a disrespectful ass nigga, how could you fuck another bitch right next to me in our bed."

"Correction my bed, you didn't buy shit in this motherfucka."

"What happened to all that, I'm gone take care of you, I'm not gone hurt you like he did?"

"They were just words, they worked like a charm huh?" Ice smiled putting on his clothes.

"Nobody wants pussy everybody had nor that everyone can have, and a few niggas had you. I'm out I'm about to go find me some new pussy and some blow."

"Fuck you and this punk ass house, your dope fiend ass won't be here long no way," I yelled to him as he left out the door. I was fed up I couldn't stay here any longer and take his shit. I lay on the couch and I thought of a plan, I knew I had to get on the blade and make some money. I wasn't thrilled about it but hey, some chicks screwed men and got nothing in return, at least I will be getting paid for it. I looked around his place, the place I called home for the last 8 months, I knew this life was coming to an end. I was headed back to the gutter; the gritty streets of Compton, the hub city.

I woke up bright and early and started packing my stuff, I was ready to get far from here. I only packed clothes that I could use on the daily. The others where materialistic and could be bought again. I was almost done when I heard the keys in the door. I was hoping I would be able to leave when he wasn't there. But in he walked with two chicks on his arm. His eyes told me he was high, he had a half empty bottle of Jack Daniels in his hands. The two tired looking chicks with him were holding him up, here he downed me for being a hoe; yet he had two white ones on his arms. I didn't have much fight left in me to deal with him. I was thru and fed up with him they could have him and his drug habit.

"What's good Kandi? Where you going? I hope to make some fuckin' money."

"I'm leaving."

"If you not leaving to go get me some money, you not going, a damn place."

"I'm leaving and getting as far away from your fuckin' ass, go fuck how many bitch's you want, you fuckin' dope fiend."

The look in Ice's eyes was something I had never witnessed from him. "You can leave hoe, cause I don't even want your ass no more, but if you leaving here, then your raggedy ass leaving the same way you came in." Ice leaped towards me swinging wild punches to my face. I tried to fight him back but he moved to fast the drugs had his adrenaline pumping like he was super man. We tussled all over the room, I finally was able to get on top of him, and I clung him. He shook trying to shake me off of him, just as he was about to ram me into the wall. I used my teeth, clamping down on the side of his face. I could feel my teeth, breaking into his skin and the taste of blood.

"Ugggggh!" Ice yelled. The harder he swung my body, I dug deeper. Ice used everything in him, running us into the glass mirror attached to the bedrooms closet. I let my grip on his face go, everything went black for a second. Then I felt strong punches to my body.

"Bitch, you bit me. I took you off the streets, saved your fucking life. I should have let them niggas keep you that fuckin' night. I gave you a life you would never know without me. So you leaving me, only in a fucking body bag." Ice yelled like a mad man as he continued to beat me into a bloody pulp. I became numb, I blanked out and fell unconscious.

When I finally woke up three weeks had passed and I was restrained to a hospital bed. When I was released from the hospital, due to them never finding out about my age, I went to the apartment the locks had been changed and the windows were boarded up. I walked the streets with no destination in sight, I was trying to make sense of my life and why I had been born. I found my way towards the blade, there wasn't much traffic out. The faces that were out, I didn't recognize.

I made my way to a little hole in the wall gambling shack, Ice and his friend's often hung there. I walked up and as usual there was dudes hanging outside.

"Hey is Mack around?"

"He around back, you Ice lady huh?" One of the dudes in the crowd asked, I could remember his face from some of the parties we attended.

"Something like that," I said to him. Walking pass the group of guys who stared at me, I walked inside and had to bypass the cloud of smoke. I could hear Mack's loud mouth, so I followed where the voice led me. He was in a dice game, so I waited until he finished to get his attention.

"Mack," I called out gaining his attention.

"Hey, what's good Kandi? Where you been girl?"

"In the hospital, I was just released today. Where yo' boy at?"

"You ain't heard?" Mack asked studying my face.

"Heard what?" I asked looking him dead in his face.

"Ice overdosed, somebody sold him some bad dope. He owed a lot of people, rumor is the dope laced with acid was given to him on purpose. That shit, busted my nigga heart."

I couldn't help the tears that fell from my eyes, yeah I know he beat my ass. Let me get raped and more. Yet a small part of me was sad, sad that he died that way. I knew the drugs would bring him death, he was too far gone on them.

"Damn."

"But what brings you by Kandi? What can I help you with?"

"I was coming to see if you knew where Ice was, I'm homeless."

"I can let you hold something, until you get on your feet."

"Thanks, but I'm good. I don't want to owe anyone, and I don't know when I would be able to give it back."

"I will give you the money in exchange for something."

"I don't have anything to give you Mack, I'm broke and homeless, and I don't have shit."

Mack grabbed my hand, leading me towards the back. He dropped a hundred dollars on the floor, next he dropped his pants.

"A favor for a favor."

I hesitated, he was Ice best friend. I looked from Mack's thick dick back to the money on the ground, I needed it I was starving. I dropped to my knees and served him a dose of Kandiland, I was back. I finished, grabbed the money and walked out. Turning my first trick in almost a year, yet it felt like I had never left.

Chapter 8

She hit the backseat, cause Rosa Parks never a factor, when she topping off Police.
-Kendrick Lamar

My first day back on the blade when I was released from the hospital felt wired. I knew I would have to adapt fast, back to the lifestyle. I had no other choice, only this time I was going to be playing by my own rules. I didn't have any clothes everything I had was lost in the condo. I hit the block and made my way into the swap meet, I browsed around looking for an easy target. I saw a crowd of young loud girls walk into a store the Chinese woman hawked after them, not paying me any mind. I grabbed as many clothes as I could and exited praying she hadn't saw me. I slipped into the nearest restroom and sorted through the clothes looking for something I could fit and maneuver in. I stepped out the restroom in a multi-color striped spandex dress, and transformed from Kandi into Kandiland, a girl who was all about her dollars. I hit the block; it was live with working girls walking up and down the blade. The traffic was heavy. I wanted to stay under the radar, but I knew that would only work for so long. I wasted no time getting to the money and doing me. It was the only way I was going to eat and starve wasn't something I was willing to do. I had fifty dollars left from the money I got from Mack. I used the other half on a room the previous night and on food. Within minutes I caught my first trick, it lasted 5 minutes and I walked away with a hundred dollars.

It was instilled in me, when you have a service or goods that you know are profitable and someone else wants them. You set a high price bargaining with them until you are satisfied with the offer. I wasn't taking anything less then a Ben Frank to sex me, it was that or better.

I was only 16 but life had me feeling twice my age, and this lifestyle didn't have an age. A hoe was a hoe no matter her age. Being young or old didn't matter, you was still a hoe when you out their pounding the Pavement. I had to provide for myself, and I was gone hustle those men until their pockets where dry.

"Kandiland," I heard someone call from behind me as I got out of a car.

"What's good?" it was Bam.

"Shit, out here trying to make it, what you doing out here? Everybody was rooting for you,

you got away from these streets. I heard about your boyfriend, sorry for your loss."

"Girl its cool, I'm good, just out here trying to survive."

"Survive? That nigga didn't leave you no money?"

"Girl stop listening to these people, he didn't have no money. It's much more then they out here telling. Let's just say life with him, wasn't too much better then this."

Two cars pulled up right in time. I didn't want to talk about the bullshit I went through with Ice, I wanted to just leave it where it was. That chapter was dead, just like him. I hopped into one car and Bam in the other.

After hours of jumping into car after car I was tired. I made my way towards the Spot. I stopped in my tracks as I replayed the last time I took this walk. I looked around to see if I seen anyone paying attention to me, there was no one out of the ordinary so I kept walking. I made it to the Spot, Akbar; the manger was in the booth with his eyes glued on the porno in front of him as he pulled on his limp penis.

"Ugh, you are so damn nasty Akbar."

"Uh, oh hey Kandiland," Akbar said straightening his pants. "I haven't seen you around these parts in a while."

"I know, but I'm back. I need a room." Akbar smiled a flirty grin, I already knew what he wanted. "Hell no, I'm not fucking you, neither am I going to suck your dick, so forget it."

"What you have against Thee Akbar?"

"Akbar, I don't have nothing against your freaky ass, I'm just not giving you no ass, forget it. Now can I get a room, my feet hurt and I need a shower."

"Okay, but Thee Akbar gone get a taste of Thee Kandiland one day, room 3 for you."

"Thanks Akbar, and don't tell anyone I'm here."

"Will do Kandiland."

Akbar went back to watching the porno in front of him. I walked down the hall to the end where room 3 was. The sounds of pleasure could be heard, and the smell of stank pussy could be smelled a mile away. Some women never left the rooms, their tricks came to them.

The Spot wasn't hardly nice at all but it was better than nothing. I couldn't deny, I had gotten accustom to the finer things in life that Ice had provided for me, but the cost that came with it wasn't hardly worth it. It felt like I started at the bottom and tried to reach the top only to land right back where I started.

I showered in the rusty shower and laid down to catch a couple of hours of sleep before the night shift started. The night shift you made more money, but the risk was greater. It was more pimps out lurking and the police patrolled like crazy looking for freebies or just to cause trouble.

After a three-hour nap, I felt rejuvenated and ready to get to the money. I dressed into another dress I got from the store earlier that day, and made my way down the street to the block. It was Friday night and payday, the weekends were the best. Traffic flowed of horny drunken men wanting to feel something wet and tight. Just as I was making my way into the shopping center a car, a police car cut me off. It was Officer Tulsa, a big sloppy white man who loved messing with the working girls for freebies.

"Get in," he said to me never making eye contact with me.

"For what? Am I under arrest or something?"

I had never had an encounter with Tulsa, but had heard many stories from the other girls about him.

"You must not know who I am?"

"You're a police officer, is there anything special I am supposed to know about you?"

"Well you better ask and learn quickly about me. Now get in the car before I haul your ass off to the station."

"On what charges? I'm just walking down the street, this is harassment."

"I've been watching you since earlier, you're a hoe like the rest of these bitches out here. Now you can either give me what I want or I can take your young ass to the holding tank and make your parents come get you, and find out what your ass is up to."

I knew he was bluffing, he just wanted some for free. I would have stood my ground if it were someone else, but Tulsa was known to get aggressive when he wanted something. I got into the backseat and he pulled off.

"What do you want?"

"I want it all."

"And how much money do you have?"
Tulsa laughed "I'm not paying you shit, and you better not half ass service me either."
Tulsa pulled up to an abandoned apartment complex and instantly pulled out his pudgy penis from his pants.

"You can start off with sucking my dick bitch."
I climbed over the seat and followed his orders trying to hurry, so I could be done with him. Within minutes he was climaxing and moaning. I was thankful a call came through so he wouldn't ask for anything else.

"You my bitch now, when I pull up or you see me. You just get in, I don't give a fuck what you are doing, now get out I have business to handle."

"Yeah whatever," I said getting out the car.

"You gone learn bitch," Tulsa said pulling off.
I walked the short distance back to the blade and pranced up and down the street catching a few more cars. I was beyond tired and the cheap heels I had on had my feet numb. I was headed back to The Spot when Tulsa pulled along side of me.

"Where you going?"
I didn't answer him, I just kept walking as if I didn't hear him. I knew it would piss him off. I

didn't owe him anything and didn't have time for him, or any other man who wanted to control me. Tulsa sped off and I was beyond thankful. I just wanted to get to the room and brush my teeth and shower.

I made it to the Spot only to find Tulsa squad car parked and him and Akbar engaging in a conversation. I knew Akbar gave me up, he didn't mess with the police because of his shady wrong doings. I walked past the men like I didn't know them.

"I see you didn't get the memo, I run shit around here."

"What do you want from me now?"

Tulsa didn't respond, so I walked off headed to the room. I stripped from my clothing and headed towards the shower. Just as I stepped a foot into the shower the room door flew open and in walked Tulsa.

Tulsa stormed my way, he brushed his large frame against me pinning me up against the wall.

"So you a little disrespectful ass bitch!" Tulsa said flinging my body onto the bed.

"Open up."

"Nah, fuck you. This is rape."

"Bitch you fuck for a living, you like it. Now open up or I'm gone take it, and you're not gone do shit about it."

I opened my legs, Tulsa pulled down his pants and pulled out his pudgy pink meat. Gripping my legs he slid inside of me and began to pound away. I lay on the bed hoping he finished fast, he wasn't working with much so I knew he wouldn't hang long. Tulsa grunted as sweat started to pulsate from his pores.

"Yeah! Yeah!. Fuck this pussy is good, I know you making money off this shit" he moaned. I couldn't look him in his face, or even pretend like I liked it, like I did with my other tricks. It wasn't long when Tulsa pulled out and released his hot sticky load onto my leg.

"That was some good shit, better than I had in the last few days. Now don't forget what I told your ass," Tulsa walked out the door. I knew that was the start of an ugly situation and would only get worst by time. I showered and climbed into the bed. Being back on the blade was going to show me more about life than I had ever known.

Chapter 9

Fancy girls, on Long Beach Blvd. Flagging down all of these flashy cars
                              - Kendrick Lamar

"What the Blvd looking like?" I asked as soon as I stepped in front of a little store in the shopping center where I saw Jazz.

"It's kind of dry out here, the boy's been hot. They picked up Shae-Shae and Bam up like an hour ago," Jazz said.

Jazz was a thick big booty Redbone who worked the blade all over. I met her a few years back when I was introduced to the world of pimping. Jazz grew up in the foster care system and moved around a lot and had been through a lot. She landed on the blade after she started to mess with a dude trying to make ends meet to feed her children. Her children's father had just got knocked and was sentenced to prison on major drug charges. The dude turned out to be a pimp. He willed her right to the streets. She fell for him and wanted to please him, so she did

everything he asked, including selling her body.
She turned out to be his biggest moneymaker,
leaving her with an addiction to money, sex and
coke. She grew to love the lifestyle, so after
getting her children took by her children's father
family. All she cared about was getting high and
making Tank's money.

She had 10 years down on the blade and
knew everything there was to know about the
life. She always looked out for me because I
was young and also happened to be the very
same age as her oldest daughter, who she wasn't
there for because of the life she lived. She gave
me a lot of wisdom on the streets and the in and
outs of what the life was about. She wanted me
to get far away from this life, but I was trapped;
I couldn't see any other vision besides using
what I had to make money. I mean I tried and he
didn't work, this was my life I was born into it.
People didn't understand that the game and
lifestyle was more than the naked eye could see.
I was deep in a life style that came with rules,
regulations, boundaries and consequences. We
work 7 days a week, there was no vacations, no
sick days and you can skip me time; it was all
about the chase of that almighty dollar. I had
been back on the blade for a month since the
incident with Ice. Every day was a constant
duck and dodge for me, from other pimps trying
to boss up on me, to the police trying to fuck for
free or arrest me.

Jazz and I were making small talk when a
dark colored truck pulled in front of us. The

windows were tinted so we couldn't see inside. The car sat there for a moment before the front window rolled down.

"Kandiland" the driver called out, a light brown skinned man said with shades over his eyes.

"Who are you?" I asked not moving from where I stood.

"Blaque sent me, get in the back."

"Nah, he wants me tell him to come too me, I'm not about to get in the car with you. I don't know you," I said to the driver. He picked up the phone and made small talk, I couldn't hear what he was saying but the change in his face let me know he didn't like the orders he had just been given.

"I don't want to harm you, but you need to get into this car or I'm gone put you in this car the choice is yours. Blaque just wants to talk to you."

"Just go Kandiland, you don't want to get on Blaque's bad side. I will be here waiting on you and if you're not back in 2 hours I'm calling the police." Jazz said to me in a hushed tone. Blaque's name rang on the streets as being a ruthless pimp and hustler, I knew in due time someone was going to court me. I jumped into the backseat as the driver sped out the shopping center.

I wasn't familiar with the small cities outside of my regular daily landmarks, the ride wasn't far and was filled with quietness. We pulled up to a modest two-story house.

"We here," the driver said unlocking the door. I got out and waited for him.

"Follow me," he said.

I followed him inside the house. "Have a seat Blaque will be out." I took a seat on one of the couches. The room was all white with leather furniture.

It felt like I was waiting for forever. My palms began to get sweaty, I didn't know how this would turn out. I fidgeted with my hands when a tall lanky dark skin man walked into the room, in nothing but a silk robe. I didn't know what Blaque looked like, I had only heard about him.

"So you are the infamous Ms. Kandiland that's out there giving these others girls the blues and having these niggas turn they shit down, just to wait on you."

"What can I say, I was taught well."

"Yeah by Big and his Bitch?"

"Yeah Madam"

"Back in the day they called her Choc, because of her chocolate skin. You look a lot like her, that's your mother correct?"

"The bitch gave birth to me, I wouldn't call her a mother."

"Well, I really don't care too much about that. What's the deal with Big and you jumping ship?"

"They put me out, so I bounced and did shit on my own."

"Then you was with Ice, before he passed?"

"Yeah, he saved my life. I was in the midst of being kidnapped and he saved me. But I messed with him on another level than getting money."

"You were his bitch, right?"

"Something like that, we lived together and fucked on the regular. But why you asking me so many questions about Ice? He dead. You know a lot about me."

"That's my job, when I am interested in something. I have to find out everything that I need to know about them."

"Interested? Who? You?"

"I know you out there with no back-up, so I will make you a proposition. You can get down with me and I will insure you, you will make more money than you ever did with Big."

"And if I choose not to get down with you?"

"You won't make a dollar on them streets, I'm connected. As you can see I found you and know everything I need to know about you."
I sat there looking at him; I liked the freedom of being my own boss, keeping all of my money. But he was right I was out there with no backup and was an easy target.

"The choice is yours."

"Okay, I will get down with you."

"Good choice, now come over here and show me what these niggas out here waiting around for."
Blaque opened his silk robe and his hardened erect penis stood at an attention. I walked in front of him and took him into my mouth and

utilized my tongue up and down his long manhood until he erupted. I climbed on top of him and rode him until we both climaxed.

"There is a bathroom to your right, go get cleaned up so I can take you to meet the others girls and where you will be living now, then you can get back to making money."

I went into the restroom to clean myself up. I returned back to the room, Blaque had left to change. I sat and waited for him to return.

We pulled up to another house, it was nice and very big, it wasn't as nice as Blaque but it was nice.

"This is where you will be living from now on, I know you been crashing at the Spot."

"Okay, who all lives here?"

"Your new sisters. This is a six-bedroom house; there are 2 girls to a room. Follow me so you can meet the girls that are here."

We walked into the house, it was quiet for so many women to occupy the space. It was clean and smelled fresh. Blaque made a funny noise with his mouth that resembled the sound of a bird. Women rushed down the long steep wrap around stairs.

"Remember that call, when you hear it. It means you need to get to me and do it quickly."

"Taz, this is Kandiland. She will be your new roommate show her where she will be living. The rest of you bitch's meet Kandiland. She not new to the game so don't start with that messy shit. Y'all have an hour to get ready for those who are about to be on duty, a car will be

here, so have your asses ready. I'm out,
Kandiland you gon' have the 12-8 shift, but get
ready you going out early with the rest of these
bitches."
With that Blaque was back out the door.

"Come this way," Taz said.
I followed her upstairs bypassing room's that
had their doors open, the rooms were nice.

"This is your new living quarters, you can
take that bed over there." Taz pointed to a queen
size slay bed that was up against the wall. "This
half is your closet space, this is the restroom.
You clean the restroom after every use."

"How does it go with food and space?"
There are two fridges one in the kitchen and one
in the garage, Blaque has someone come and
shop for food. That food is for everyone. If you
want your own knick nacks then you have to
buy them on your own and write your name on
them. It's still a chance one of these bitch's can
eat it while you gone."

"How long have you been living here?"

"I've been here 3 months, I hate it and these
bitches are messy, Blaque is cool. One of the
best pimps I've had. Just do what he says or be
ready to get your ass beat."

"Okay."

"Oh, and none of these bitch's are your
friends. They will throw you under the bus
faster then you can blink your eyes. So words of
advice keep to yourself."

"I'm not new to this, I've been on the streets
for a while I know how to handle myself and

these chicks, but thanks."

"No problem, there is new clothes in the closet, you better start getting ready."
I really didn't understand Taz and her attitude, but I wasn't there to make any new friends. I was cool with the chicks I had already established a bond with. I was there to get money and if they couldn't produce those dead presidents I could care less about what they were going through. I sorted through the closet full of clothes and shoes that still had price tags on them. I found a cute short Maxi dress with a pair of platforms in my size. I showered quickly and was ready as soon as the car pulled up.

When I made it back to the Blade I looked for Jazz, to let her know I was okay.

"Have y'all seen Jazz?" I asked the small huddle of women.

"She left with a trick about an hour ago," one of the women said. I hadn't seen her around before.

"Well if you see her let her know Kandiland is looking for her."

"I will."

"Thanks," I said to her before walking off. The shopping center had become full of traffic due to all the shops inside. I stood to the side of the building watching the flow of traffic. It was funny how the tricks would search for you if you weren't visible to them when they passed. I saw a truck drive up and down 3 times never stopping to pick up any of the girls. I walked to the sidewalk just as he made his way back down the street for the fourth time.

The truck pulled on the side of me.

"Hola Hermosa, quiero foller contigo.

I didn't understand what the man was asking but I did know that there was only one thing he could want. My Spanish was bad but I knew how to ask what I needed to know.

"Quiere Cono?"

"Si, Si."

"Tienes dinero?"

"Si."

"Eres la Policia?"

"No la Policia."

Most didn't like taking the Mexican men because most of them didn't speak English, where as I learned the basic information I needed from them. If they wanted pussy, had money and were they the police. I loved the Mexican men more then anyone. They were packed small and easy to please. Black men were hung like a horse, and even though the pleasure was good. After fucking more then one man in a day, you wanted something quick and easy. Black men were cheap and wanted too much for nothing. The white men paid the price but were too freaky and wanted the weirdest forms of sexual acts.

I got into the car and we were off, in less than ten minutes I was finished and back on the blade with another hundred in my pocket and he was happy and on his way home to his wife. The night started to fall and like they say the freaks come out at night, the flow of traffic was

busy giving me the chance to make an
impression on Blaque with doubling my
minimum of $500.00 for the night.

"Kandiland, I see you about your paper, I
like that. You chose up once, don't make it a
habit. Cause with me you will lose your life. Go
get some rest."

I walked away from Blaque and felt his every
word, I knew he was speaking the truth.

Chapter 10

It had been almost two months since the day I agreed to be down with Blaque. Since I had been kicked out, I hadn't crossed paths with Big and Madam, I knew in due time it would happen. We ran in the same circle, every day I looked and prepared for him to show up. There were rules and regulations in this life and I crossed a few by being on the blade getting the next man's bread. Big was the one who introduced me to this life, my loyalty to him should always remain. If not then he couldn't be liable for his actions. Big was a ruthless old head in the game, he had gained a lot of respect in the game from all over. There wasn't a track or blade that made money that Big didn't know of in California.

I knew in due time I would run into them or one of their hoes who was loyal to them out on the blade. Madam had worked the blade for years and still had pull on information. A ton of chicks that didn't like me got down with them. A few of them worked on the Blvd on a regular.

I always saw them but I stayed out their way, I didn't want the stress and drama from Big.

The sun was beaming, it was such a beautiful day in the city. There wasn't much work, the blade had been dry for the last hour. There wasn't any use for me to just be standing around, there wasn't any money to be made. So, I decided to go into the nail shop in the shopping center and get myself a pedicure hoping traffic would pick up by the time I was through. Life had been different with Blqaue, never had I been giving my own money. With Big all money went to him I didn't see any of it. Ice never gave me money, he just spent it on me. Blaque gave us, a weekly allowance to up keep ourselves. It was a must you looked the part of an actress, or singer when you were down with his team. Blaque's stable of women could be pinpointed, because we stood out.

Blaque was a ruthless hustler, he got his start on the street pushing drugs, and then he got into pimping. His only care was his money, and finding each way he could get it. He had 50 girls in his stable spreading from the Blvd, Fig, and Sunset all the way to Orange County. He even had male hoes, some were into men other were strictly women.

Many hated Blaque, he only associated himself with the best and had requirements to get down with his crew. He wanted the best looking women out there on the blade attached to his name. Every one of his women was handpicked by him and had to go through him before they were able to rep his name. His motto was *"The better the Bitch looked, the more money the hoe can make."* Everyone in his stable, he had sexed some on the regular. It was a part of him selecting you, good sex brought in money. If you didn't sex him good enough you weren't worthy of being on his team, because you couldn't bring him any money.

When I was done with getting my pedicure I made my way down the Blade, traffic had picked up lightly. The corner workers had received their pay and were looking to spend some on something tight and wet, and I was ready to service them and collect the money. I crossed the street as a Red Benz coupe reared in front of me. His eyes watched me as I made my way to the other side of the street. I made eye contact with him, but couldn't hold it. My eyes caught something else; it was Starr; Big's girlfriend and bottom bitch. My dislike for her was a reflection of my hatred towards Big and Madam. The feeling was mutual, she didn't care for me. She felt Big gave me special attention, she didn't like that. She was his bottom bitch; she was supposed to get the special treatment, alongside Madam. She didn't care that he helped create me, to her I was just another young hoe in his stable of bitches that wanted to replace her. We were often compared, because of our dark skin. She hated how everyone complimented me on my smooth heresy chocolate skin, light brown dopey shaped eyes, full lips and silky jet-black hair. Star was the opposite, short, dark as tar and pudgy and still sported a blonde wig, like Julia Roberts, in pretty women.

At 17 my body had developed well, five years of turning tricks made my body look like a woman twice my age. A perky set of 38 D cup breast, a flat stomach and my long bowlegs drove the men crazy. I didn't have much in the back, but I had enough. I was often told I was pretty, sometimes I thought it was all about getting what they needed. Some days I felt pretty and other days, I felt regular. I tried to stay in my own lane, got out there did me and made my money, that's what it was about, getting money.

"I heard what happened to your boyfriend, that sexy ass nigga Ice. That shit was sad, he was doing his thang with that rapping shit. Until that nigga started fucking with that shit, heard he was letting niggas run in his ass for that shit. Word around here, he overdosed on dope. He had you over there thinking you were better then us, but we see that wasn't true. Cause' you back where you started." Starr said, hawking me up and down. She had on her normal tired attire, spandex dress, and clear heels.

"Once a hoe, always a hoe; remember that. No matter how many times you leave, you gone find your way back, you're not shit, never will be just like the rest of us. Nigga played captain save a hoe and fucked around and got strung out, and died. These niggas better learn to leave them rotten pussy bitches alone," Starr said with a chuckle.

My blood was boiling at this point. I stared back at Starr putting on a show for her little crew. Years later she still wore blonde hair, like it was the thing to do. She looked worst than a two-dollar crack hoe, jonein' for her next hit.

"Let us get some facts straight bitch. I don't know what the fuck that man was out there doing, I can careless he made his bed now his ass laying 6 feet under in that muthafucka', I don't think I'm better than the next bitch, you think I'm better then you. That's your problem, not mine; deal with it. With your ole' washed up ass". I resorted, glaring at her and the rest of the chicks behind her. "Better be glad I'm having a good day or I'd fuck you up. Remember I'm still that bitch, I beat your ass once and I won't hesitate to do it again."

"Whatever bitch just remember the rules. Oh and I will let Big and The Madam know your doing well, really well from the looks of it, getting down with Blaque and all." Starr looked at me from head to toe.

"Fuck you and them, now move out my way before I fuck you and the rest of these tired looking ass hoes up," I sneered.
I pushed through the crowd that started to form looking for a girl fight. It wasn't uncommon to see two hoes outside fighting. That brought attention, which I wasn't looking for, and Blaque didn't tolerate. Big and his bitch were the last people I wanted to run into, I knew it would be any day with big mouth ass Starr. I couldn't just let that tramp step to me. I had to

let her know. I thought to myself as I walked off. I knew I had to let her and the rest of the hoes out there know I wasn't to be messed with just because I was young. I turned around and marched back up to her, she was still standing around, showing out for the crowd. Using my backhand, I slapped Starr sending her flying to the concrete.

"Don't forget to tell them that too, bitch!" I started to strike her again. *"Fuck it"* I said to myself. I had money to make or get my ass beat. So I left Starr alone, laying on the concrete, with a small hurdle surrounding her. I put on my game face and went back to the money.

After a few hours of jumping in and out of cars and meeting some of my regulars, I was ready to go shower and lay down. I had done my eight hours and made my minimum plus extras. I knew Blaque was lurking around or had someone watching us. We were all issued cell phones from Blaque that had tracking information on all of us that was transmitted to Blaque.

"Daddy I got money for you, I'm ready to head to the house until later, it's dry."

"Where you at?"

"Murray," I said into the phone as my eyes was watching the police squad car riding pass slowly. They gave me a long stare, letting me know they thought I was up to something. "The boys hot, they watching me now."

"Be there in 5 minutes, stay low," Blaque replied before ending the call.

I waited for Blaque in the cut, trying to stay out of the view of the police.

Within minutes Blaque pulled up in his all Black Range Rover, with the music blasting. The police had disappeared, I hopped in the backseat and he pulled off. We never exchanged money in front of the other girls, chicks hated to see you pulling in more money than they brought in. So Moe, Blaque's younger brother only did it in private.

Moe's Camaro was parked in the driveway, awaiting on our arrival. I waited until the girl before me stepped from the car.

"Hey Moe, this what I got." I handed Moe the money.

"What's good Kandiland? How much money you got for me?"

"A stack."

"Damn, you be about your paper?"

"Damn right, you know Blaque don't play that shit. So I'm out there getting it by all means necessary, doing me"

"And you do you, very well; pretty lady." Moe said with a small grin on his face.

I found Moe attractive, I had become distinct to the male species. They were all the same to me, all they wanted to do was fuck you and control you. It was something else about Moe, I just couldn't put my finger on it. Moe kept a fresh low caesar cut. He was 5'10 his body was ripped and covered with Ink, tattoos itched into his skin that made him even more appealing to the eye. He always looked and smelled nice. Moe was twenty years old and an all-star running back for UCLA. To keep him out of trouble Blaque made him work close to him. He was in charge of collecting the money and keeping the books, the money was to only be given to him.

When I was around Moe I couldn't control the butterflies in my stomach, I was attracted to him. Every time I was around him it hit me. I was still a child, even though I was out there in the big world carrying myself as a woman, inside I was a child. I had a major crush on my pimp's brother. I was skilled in feeling a man's vibe, I felt the vibe from him he wanted me as well. Something that couldn't ever happen on each of our parts.

"Kandiland I hope you don't get offended by this, but I think you're beautiful."

The butterflies doubled inside my stomach hearing him refer to me in that way. Most called me a bad bitch, sexy but never beautiful, Ice had in the past, but it leaving Moe's mouth, I felt it.

"Thanks Moe, you not so bad on the eyes yourself."

"Thanks, can I ask you a personal question?"

"Shoot" I was nervous. I didn't know what sort of personal question he wanted to ask me.

"How did you get out here, like this?"

"It's a long story."

"Well we can grab a bite to eat, and we can talk about it."

"This is all I was taught, it's the only thing I know, and it's the only thing I'm good at."

"It's never too late to learn and master

something else."

"I gotta go Moe, we can't do this. Blaque will fuck us both up, we are both crossing the line and I'm not worth fuckin' up you and your brother's relationship."

I got up and ran upstairs to my room and locked myself inside. Taz was still out on the streets, so I had the room to myself. I stripped and went to take a shower.

Just as I got back into the room my phone was ringing.

"Hello?"

"What the fuck took you so fuckin' long too answer the phone bitch!" Blaque spat into the phone.

"I went to shower, after Moe finished the count."

"Yeah okay bitch, get some rest. I need you out there tonight, I got a new little bitch I need you to watch after."

"I'm tired, can you get someone else do it?"

"Bitch, did I ask someone else to do it?"

"No"

"Then have yo' black ass ready at nine"

"Okay Daddy, but can I go on Western or Fig? The Blvd kind of dry."

"I don't give a fuck where you go, just be on one of them muthafuckas'. Check in with Honey when you touch down. I'm gone be busy so I will send a car."

"Okay."

After taking a much-needed nap I woke up and made me some pork flavor ramen noodles and grabbed a nice cold pineapple soda. I still had some time to kill, so I put a movie into the DVD player. I laid back and tried to focus on the screen but my mind drifted to Moe. He was so sexy to me, I wonder if he was packing like his brother or better below the waist. I pushed the thoughts into the back of my mind and focused on the TV screen in front of me, and decided what I would wear for the night.

Chapter 11

I heard Blaque's loud music and him lying on the horn, *"thought this nigga was sending a car" I thought to myself.* I grabbed my purse and rushed out the door. I got into the car; Blaque was on the phone and didn't acknowledge me at first.

"What's good Kandiland? You looking mighty sexy tonight, who you trying to impress?"

"Hey Daddy, nobody. Just trying to get this money." I didn't ask why he came rather than the car that was supposed to pick me up.

"That's right, that's my girl. Now come service Daddy some of that tongue before we pick up this new bitch."

I unbuckled my seat belt and positioned myself with my ass high into the air, and my head in his lap as he drove. I unzipped the zipper on the 501's he wore, his chocolate pole sprang out ready for some royal Kandiland lick down. I started with the tip of his chocolate pole, flickering my tongue over the slit before taking just the tip into my mouth. I used my hands to massage his balls and the base of his shaft, sucking on his tip hard. I sucked harder and harder until a moan escape his lips. With one hand he pushed my head down, sliding him into my mouth. I gripped him as I went up and down. I started slowly then faster until my head bobbed up and down his pole, gently he slid down my throat. He gripped my hair tighter as he fucked my mouth. He pulled the car into a parking stall, using both hands he guided my head up and down his pole until he was on the verge of rupture.

"Come give Daddy a ride."

Doing as I was told, I pushed my dress above my hips, straddled his lap and slid his massive hardened penis inside. I adjusted my self on his penis, making sure he was deep inside. I placed my hands on the dashboard and started twisting my hips .Blaque thrusted his pelvic back into me making me bounce up and down. Blaque was hung, but as I sat with his penis inside of me I couldn't help but think of Moe, my mind drifted to Moe's face and before I knew it I was riding Blaque fast then slow. I was lost into wanting to please Moe, more than Blaque that I went wild.

"Yeah bitch, ride that dick" Blaque encouraged. If he knew what was on my mind, I would be dead. I didn't say anything I just smiled and continued to let my ass collide with his thighs until he was at his peak. I climbed off of him and sucked him into my mouth catching his cum just as it shot out, letting the warm liquid slide down my throat. I grabbed my bag and pulled out the summers eve feminine wipes and cleaned him off, he tucked his penis back into his pants. I quickly wiped myself up and rinsed my mouth with the mouthwash in my purse.

Five minutes later we pulled up to one of the Motels where Blaque ran a lot of his business. He laid on the horn and out came a pretty redbone chick with fire engine hair down to her ass. She was clad in some coochie cutters and a half tank, and red chucks were on her feet. Blaque rode down the window.

"Get in, Redd this Kandi. She will be going over some of my rules, pay attention because you will be out there alone tomorrow and I don't tolerate fuck ups."

"Okay," she said popping some gum. She was young, younger then I was. I wondered how she crossed paths with Blaque. I hope she knew what she had just signed up for, because with Blaque there was no turning back. Only escape from him was jail or death.

"Either I will be or someone will be around watching incase you need any thing, have a good night," Blaque said to us as he pulled up to the curb, hit the locks and let us out the car.

"Okay," we said in unison stepping from the car. The streets weren't so busy for a Saturday night on Western Ave.

"Okay, pay attention because I will only go over something once, you don't understand say it now. I will not be responsible for any of your fuck ups so make sure you get it right."

"Got'cha."

"As you can see this is Western, not many chicks work this block like that, unless the others are hot. There are some regular chicks that work this line daily. Some of them are cool, while others don't give a shit about you. It's a part of the game, you out here to make money not friends so pay them no mind, understand?"

"Yeah I understand, try and keep to yourself much as possible, we in the money making business; not friends."

"Good, I just might like you. Now you know you never make direct eye contact with another pimp. Believe everything you hear about Blaque so converse with these pimps as less as possible, try not at all. Watch the chicks you converse with, some are out here trying to take you home with them, for their pimp. That's like signing your papers out this bitch."

"Okay, but what if they say they trying to catch a date?"

"Pay attention to your surroundings, you learn cars. Then you will be able to tell if he is a pimp, trick or undercover. This is a vital part of this job, lack of it can wind your ass in jail. And Blaque won't bail your ass out so take my advice. You're a fresh face so they are going to be on you, these men are clever ass hell, which means you have to stay two steps ahead to survive. If you can't handle someone, a bitch, pimp or tick. Hit Blaque and let him or one of his dudes handle it."

"Okay," Redd nodded her head. I hope she got what I said, because if she didn't she would drown in this ocean full of sharks.

"When you walk up to a car pay attention inside the car and body language. If it doesn't feel right, let the shit go. That's the same for when you do get into the car. First question you need to ask is, are you the Police? Tell them to touch you. If they can't answer that nor touch you get out the car, it's a police officer. And like I said Blaque won't bail you out and when you do get out, you will have to work twice as hard to replace any money you could have made."

"Okay, so pay attention to body language inside the car, ask if they are the police and to touch me?"

"I see you pay attention well."

"Now let's talk about prices, set high prices and negotiate to a price you feel is fair for what is being asked of you. I don't go on any dates for anything less than a hundred dollars and that's a quickie, ten minutes or less. Each additional five minutes is fifty dollars. Some of these bitches are out here all night trying to make money because they twenty dollars here, twenty dollars there. Fuck that I know my shit good, so I will charge accordingly. You should always have that mind frame. Fuck what these other broads out here doing, because when you're out here pounding the pavement, it's every hoe for themselves."

"It's much more too this then I ever knew,"

Redd said while looking around at the cars driving pass, picking up girls.

"It sure is, you look like you have a temper or sassy with the mouth. That's cool but make sure you can back it up. You will have people hollering all sorts of things your way. Some people get a kick out of driving down the street calling you names. Don't pay them any mind, you know what you out here doing and if you cool with it, then fuck it. Hell half of them fucking on everything walking and they still broke."

"Have you ever had to fight someone over them calling you a name?"

"Girl, I don't care what these people say, as long as they don't put they hands on me I'm good. Words are words they don't hurt me, I've had cruel things said to me by the ones who were supposed to love me. So those who don't know me, I can care less what they have to say, if they don't have no money for me, fuck them."

"Okay, so what about the police over here?"

"The police over here know this is a major street for prostitution so they are extremely hot, so pay attention because they be itching to take you in. There is some who will act like they are going to take you to jail in front of everyone, just so you can beg them not to. In the end all they want is some free pussy, they are the crookest bastards."

"Do you have any police officers as regulars?"

"Yeah this one asshole, but don't worry

about getting them as a regular cause they won't ever pay, you been doing good so you have the next car. Don't fuck this up Redd."

"Okay."

A car pulled up to the curb just a little passed us, the man was wearing a cap, and using his hand out the window he signaled for one of us to come over.

"That's you Redd."

Redd walked the short distance to the passenger side window of the car, the window was down letting her stick her head inside. Just as she was told she looked around the car quickly. Her smile quickly turned from the sexy grin she once possessed into a frown as she backed away from the car and headed back my way.

"What's wrong?" I asked her looking back at the car behind her.

"He wants you."

"Who the fuck is that, I don't know that car."

"Girl I don't know, but he told me to send your black ass over."

I didn't have regulars on Western, because I didn't come this way that often. So I didn't know what to expect of someone looking for me. I was slightly nervous. "Fuck it" I said to myself as I stormed to the car. Easing my head into the passenger's window I was surprised to see no other than Officer Tulsa.

"Get your black ass in this fucking car right now."

I got into the car, even though I didn't want to. I didn't want him to make a scene, something he was used to doing. I couldn't stand him, I hated to see him coming. Sometimes I would have sworn he was my pimp, instead of Blaque.

"You trying to hide from me?"

"What the fuck you talking about Tulsa?" I asked him with an annoyed attitude.

"Hoe, you heard what I said."

"I heard what you said, but why would you be thinking I'm hiding from you. I go where I am told to go."

"You a Blvd hoe, since when you start working other lines?"

"When my daddy told me I was going to be working here."

"So why didn't you call me?"

"I didn't feel the need to, you're not my Daddy."

"That nigga not your Daddy, he your pimp. That nigga Big your Daddy; shit he was your pimp too," Tulsa chuckled.

"Whatever," I said. "I'm watching over a girl, so are we done? Since I know your ass don't have no money, you're wasting my time."

"We done when I say we are done."
Tulsa pulled off without saying anything, he locked the doors and turned up the music. He didn't say anything until we pulled up to an abandoned warehouse.

"Get out."
I was scared, Tulsa wasn't predicable and we were in a secluded area. I couldn't count how many times he just pulled up on me and slapped me around. He was deranged and abusive and in

some sick way I felt he got a kick out of it.

"Tell Blaque you're my bitch, and he needs to report to me when he sends you somewhere else. I don't want to have to come looking for you, when I'm tryna' get my dick wet."

"You tell him that crazy shit. I'm not tryna get fucked up."

The back of his hand met my face so fast I couldn't move. "I see you didn't learn about that smart mouth of yours huh? I think you like me beating yo ass, huh?" Tulsa asked striking me again, this time I was prepared for it, I stepped back making him almost lose his footing. I tried to make a run for it, but he was quick.

"Where the fuck you think you going bitch?" I want you to run so I really can fuck your black ass up."

I knew he was telling the truth so I stood there and prepared myself for the beating I knew would come. I just hoped he hurried and got it over with. He pushed my body up against the cold steel doors with one hand under my neck he fumbled with his pants. Once he got his penis out, he stroked the hairy pale thing. He knew I didn't wear underwear, lifting my dress he roughly grabbed my vagina

"You like it rough huh? You like this vanilla penis inside that wet chocolate?" Tulsa asked. I didn't even try answering because my answer wouldn't be the answer he wanted, and he wouldn't like that. So I remained quiet.

He forced himself inside of me and wasted no time pumping fast inside of me. "Damn this pussy so bomb, Ahh! Shit!" he moaned. "You like this dick bitch? Tell me you like it?"

"I like it! I like it!" I yelled hoping he would stop. The burning sensation from his non-stopping pumping had me in agony. But it seemed to fuel him. He kept going, with his hands around my neck on my pressure point, I felt at any time I would give out. He pulled out and released the death grip from my neck.

"Get on your knees."
Doing as I was told I got on my knees, thinking he wanted some head.
Tulsa gripped his penis "Ahh" he moaned shooting his semen onto my face.

"Damn, that was a good nut. How my kid's taste?" Tulsa said laughing shaking his penis.
I didn't respond, I just looked at him. Tulsa couldn't have kids. So all I possibly could taste were the blanks he was shooting.

"Yeah all of them blanks" I said at a whisper. Wiping his semen from my face the best I could with the back of my hand. I refused to show him he hurt my pride. When I turned tricks I was used to being in charge. I said what went and what didn't. With Tulsa I felt like a mouse running to not be eaten by the big snake.

"Get up, get back into the car so I can drop you back off, I'm done with you for the day."
I slowly walked towards the car, the torture my vagina sustained left it throbbing in pain. The short ride back Western was filled with Tulsa singing off beat to some corny country song. We pulled up down the street from where he

picked me up from, away from the flowing traffic. I grabbed my bag prepared to get out of his car.

"Let me see this," Tulsa said snatching my bag from me.

"Can I have my fuckin' bag back?" He ignored me and continued to ram shack through it. I hope he wouldn't discover the slit at the bottom that contained the money I had tucked inside. But like I hope he wouldn't, he did.

"Looks like I came up on some quick money."

"What the fuck Tulsa, give me my money back," I snapped.

"Get out my car bitch, this is mine. Tell Blaque if he want it, come get it from me." He threw my purse back at me. "Now get out, I have a date to get ready for."

"I'm not going no damn where, until you give me my damn money back."

"Don't make me throw your ass out of my car. This is my money now. Go out there and make you some more, for your daddy. Because I'm about to take my bitch out with this," Tulsa said laughing. "Wine and dine her and get some of that exclusive pussy," he chuckled again.

I grabbed my bag, "Fuck you Tulsa, I hope that bitch don't give you shit; you little dick bastard." I yelled slamming his door and making a beeline towards traffic. Tulsa was crazy, but he wouldn't make a scene in front of everyone. I looked back and all I saw was his taillights, relieved I started to walk towards the little African store to use their restroom.

"Aye Kandiland," someone called. "That red head that came with you, went on a date about 20 minutes ago. She told me to tell you if you came back before she did."

"Cool, thanks" I said to her. China, a short Chinese girl that worked Western. She didn't speak too many, afraid of them finding out that she used to be a police officer in her hometown before being kidnapped and brought to the states. She spent many years in Mexico working as a sex slave in a whorehouse. She was bought here by her pimp three years ago and been working the streets ever since with a heavy addiction to heroin.

I made my way towards the back of the store, Taboos, the owner looked out for the working girls and let us use his restroom to change and clean up in between dates. I cleaned myself up quick and made my way back to the Mainline to make my money for the night.

It was hours later that I was able to catch up with Redd.

"What are your pockets looking like young one?"

"I made close to 4 hundred, I went on about 5 dates," Redd said.

"That's good for your first day, I see you learn and caught on quickly. That's a good trait in this lifestyle. Let me know when you meet your minimum and I will call Blaque and let him know it's a wrap for tonight."

"Okay," Redd replied watching the cars that passed by us.

"I will get with you in a few, I have a trick coming."

"You better work, make that money."

"Make the money, don't let it make you," I recited my favorite line from the infamous Players Club movie.

We parted ways, and two hours later we met back up. I had made my minimum plus extras.

"You ready Redd?" I asked her as soon as she walked up.

"Yup, I made a little over five."

I picked up the phone to call Blaque, before I could speak my ears were filled with his lustful grunts. "We ready," I said into the phone.

"I'm a little tied up right now, give me an hour. Ahh! Shit! I'll call you back," he said disconnecting the call.

It was 3am, the police were hot and my feet were aching and he was somewhere getting his nut off. I was beyond vexed, but I couldn't show that in front of Redd, she was new, green to him and his ways.

"Blaque tied up, he said he will get here as soon as he is done."

"Okay, well there is no use in just standing around, I'm gone try and catch a few dates," Redd said.

"Do you girl," I said to her. I wasn't going on any more dates, my vagina was still sore from Tulsa and the tricks I turned. I was ready for a hot bath.

113

It was after 5am when Blaque pulled up on the empty street.

"That's Blaque, Redd lets go."

"Good, cause I am tired ass hell, and my ass is sore from this nigga who only wanted to fuck me in my ass. His dick was huge."

"Yeah, you gone have to soak and douche your ass when you do your vaginal."

"I've never douched before."

"It's cool, I will show you."

We jumped into the car, two other girls were already inside.

It didn't take long to make it to the house, Blaque was a speed devil and there wasn't much traffic out that early in the am.

We pulled up in front of the house, I saw Moe's car outside. So I knew he was inside.

"Moe in the backroom collecting money, Redd you in the room with Kandiland."

"What about Taz?"

"What about her?"

"That's who my roommate is."

"Not anymore, Taz gone forever" he smiled. "Redd's your new roommate, now get out. I have some other bitches to pick up."

I got out of the car and tried to rush into the house, so I could be the first to get counted, so Moe wouldn't go into questions about my face. Tulsa left me with a bruise on the left side of my face and my lip was busted. Just my luck Moe took all the girls before me.

"What's good Kandi?"

"Hey Moe, how are you?"

"I'm good, but what happened to your face?"

"It's nothing."

"So you just have a busted lip and a bruise on the side of your face for nothing. Either you out there fighting again, or Blaque putting his hands on you; which one is it?"

"It's nothing Moe," I said to him I knew he would question me until he got an answer.

"It's something, you just don't want to tell me. But I will find out so it's cool. What you got for me?"

"It was Tulsa," I said in a low whisper.

"What? Who is that?"

"Officer Tulsa, he pulled up on me and was mad that I wasn't on the Blvd."

"So he hit you for that? Who the fuck does he think he is?" I could see the creases on his forehead began to form, Blaque did the same when he got pissed off.

"He is the police, I tried to run, but it would have made it worst."

"Is that all he did?" Moe asked, there was a sincere look in his eyes.

I sat there and counted out the money. "It's eight hundred and forty dollars."

"Is that all Kandi?"

"No, he raped me and took my money."

"What the fuck, how much did he take?"

"He took three hundred."

"Okay, but you good right?"

"Yeah, I'm good. Just need a hot bath."

"Okay, well I have your money down. Go take a bath and take some medicine and get you some rest. I will check up on you tomorrow."

"Okay, have a good one Moe."

"You do the same Kandi."

I walked upstairs to my room, showed Redd the do's and do not's when sharing a room with me. I ran me a piping hot bubble bath and let my body soak. Since my dealings with Ice, my body craved the best of the best of Kush. I took the already rolled blunt from my purse and sparked it and let the OG purp flow down my lungs. It felt like hours had passed when I got out of the bath, I felt relaxed and ready to get some rest. I climbed into my bed and drifted off to sleep fast.

I heard the squeaky sound of the box spring and the sound of loud moans and grunts. I looked up to see Redd in the reverse cowgirl position, bouncing up and down on a long chocolate pipe; I knew that penis from miles away. I grabbed my pillow and cover and made my way downstairs to the living room. Not before I laid my eyes on the custom Gucci shoes, confirming that it was Redd and Blaque fucking. "Damn, couldn't y'all do this downstairs?" I said. Getting no answer other than, louder moans in response.

I tried to make myself comfortable on the couch, but it seemed like their moans got louder. I grabbed my ice cream that I got earlier from Rite Aide, and turned on the TV to catch reruns of Love and Hip Hop. Turning up the volume to try and drown out the sex that was going on. I got lost into the hilarious drama on the screen. I fell right back to sleep, until I felt a presence standing over me. I opened my eyes to see Blaque standing in front of me examining my bruised face and lip.

"What the fuck happened to you?"

"Tulsa, he pulled up on me and you know the rest."

"That nigga Tulsa got it bad for you hunh? Tell that nigga I'm gone need my money, putting his hands on you and shit."

"Let him tell it, you need to report to him, about my whereabouts. This is how I ended up like this because he had to search for me."

"Fuck Tulsa, you my bitch. I'm gone see him in due time, cause he getting out of hand and becoming a pain in my ass. But I'm out."

"Bye Blaque," it was Redd standing at the bottom of the stairs butt naked.

"Take your ass back up the fuckin' stairs Redd. Get your ass some rest you gone have a long day tomorrow and Kandi won't be with you."

Redd didn't say anything, she just made her way back upstairs. I could tell she was going to be a handful. She wanted Blaque, but he didn't belong to anyone. His penis only belonged to himself he just shared it often, and when he wanted you to have it. I laid back down and tried to get some rest before the other girls got up for the day.

Pounding The Pavement

Chapter 12

The blade had major traffic, it was payday and all the men were ready to cash out on their favorite pussy before heading home, to their wives. It often baffled me how most men had wives and children. Yet they couldn't resist the pussy that came with a price tag. It showed me men were all the same; cheating nasty dogs.

"You looking mighty fine today Kandiland."

"Thank you Bone."

Bone was a local hustler who hung around the shopping center slanging anything that he could get his hands on. Movies, cd's, purses, and perfume, weed if he could sale it he had it. If you needed something, Bone was your man cause he could get it. He was ugly, short and skinny with stinky corn rolls and he couldn't dress if he even tired. But Bone got a lot of respect from us because he was a sweetheart and always showed us respect, even when we turned him down.

"Kandiland when you gone let me be your man, I can treat you better than that nigga Blaque," Bone said in a hush tone. Not wanting anyone to hear him diss Blaque.

"Bone, boy gone somewhere you know Blaque will kill you."

"He don't have to know, it can be just between me and you and my sheets," Bone laughed.

"Nice try Bone, but you know what's up. You my nigga I wash your hands, you wash mine. Let's just keep it that way."

"You can't blame a brother for trying."

"You have a good day Bone," I said to him making my way through the parking lot.

"You do the same sexy, Ms. Kandiland."
I made my way through the back streets, trying to stay off of the police radar. They were out and ready to send people off to jail, and I wasn't trying to be one. I made it to the Motel where Blaque did business, it was also a crash pad for us between dates and when the police were hot. I saw Blaque's truck and Moe's car in the parking lot, I didn't want to go in the room and take a chance of being in the presence of both of them. I stood outside trying to decide if I wanted to go inside, or try to find another room that may have been empty. I heard a car pull up behind but didn't pay much attention to it. Until I heard a deep voice, a voice I would never forget. I turned my head quickly, thinking maybe my ears were playing tricks on me. But nope there he was, the Great, Big.
I rolled my eyes inhaling and exhaling, I knew it was about to be some shit. I swiftly walked towards the room Blaque always occupied, but

Big swerved the truck cutting off my path and hopped out his truck.

"What the fuck you want, Big?"

"I'm just checking on my daughter, seeing how she living."

"I don't have time for this shit, you don't give a fuck about me. So you can stop with that bullshit, and leave before shit get ugly."

"Nobody scared of Blaque, I been doing this shit, that nigga new to the game. You need to recognize that and come back home."
I started laughing "the years I spent with you were the worst of my life. I wouldn't even on my death bed bring any money in for you, consider yourself dead to me, you and them two bitches in your car." I said pointing to Starr and Madam before turning to walk off.
Big wasn't letting me go that easy, he stormed up behind me, snatching my arm and pulling my body close to his.

"GET THE FUCK OFF ME" I yelled trying to pull away from him, but he threw his 230-pound frame on me.

"Now you listen little bitch, I came here being nice but, I see you can't accept that with your hoe ass. Remember you belong to me. And you will pay for your disloyalty whether it's voluntary or involuntary, but trust you will."
Big yelled, shaking me. "Blaque won't be able to save you; I got some hot lead for his ass too."
I looked at Big with so much malice in my heart for him, my heart was black and filled with hate.

"You disgust me, just looking at your face, makes my stomach turn."

"Now it's my turn to laugh, cause I don't give a fuck how bad your stomach turns, you will see this face for the rest of your life. Which may or may not be that long, it all depends on you and your cooperation."

"I rather be dead then to be anywhere near your fat ass, you fucking child molester!" I yelled.

Big followed my statement with a smack to my face. "You better learn some fuckin' respect."

"FUCK YOU!" I yelled holding the side of my stinging face.

I tried to run away, but he was on me. Striking me with an open hand. I yelled calling Blaque's name trying to fight Big off.

"BLAQUE! BLAQUE!" I yelled hoping he would hear me, but he didn't come out. I grew tired, I couldn't fight Big back anymore. I curled up in the fetal position as he continued to strike me repeatedly.

"Big let's go before someone sees you and calls the police, Big!" Erica yelled from the car. Big didn't care, he kept striking me "I can't hear you now? Huh? What you have to say now you loose pussy bitch."

"Aye, get the fuck off her nigga," I heard a voice I couldn't make it out, but I was grateful for who ever it was.

"Stay out this shit here nigga, this bitch is my business" Big said.

"Fuck you, Kandi my business."

I finally made out the voice, it was Moe. He swung on Big. Big wasn't expecting the swing, his delay gave Moe the upper hand. Moe was younger, in better shape and he was quick with his hands giving Big a hard time. Big had become overweight and was tired, he tried to keep his balance so that he could pull out his pistol that was tucked in his waist band. He backed up from Moe's reach and quickly pulled his pistol out, backing towards his truck.

"You gone see me again youngin, believe that, this shit not over. Kandi bitch! I'm coming for you hoe, that sweet black pussy belongs to me and I will get it. Even if it's your corpses." Big got into his truck and pulled off.

"Yo', who the fuck is that nigga?" Moe asked helping me up.

"Big."

"Big?" He repeated clueless to the name.

"Yeah, my father."

"Let me get you inside," Moe carried me to the room where Blaque always was. Moe banged on the door. "Nigga open the fucking door," Moe shouted.

"Hold up shit," Blaque said from the other side. "Go answer the door," I heard Blaque say to whoever occupied the room with him. We heard the locks turn and the door opened, Honey, one of Blaque's new bitches stood with a small towel wrapped around her body. Moe bypassed her sitting me on the other bed.

"What the fuck happened to her? Yo' ass was out there popping that smart ass mouth and

somebody hands were quicker then yours huh?"
Blaque laughed as he put his clothes back on.

"Nah, some nigga ran up on her, Kandi
what was his name again?"

"Big."

"Yeah, me and that nigga was locking until
he pulled a piece out on me."

"He pulled a gun out on you?"

"Didn't I just say that Bro? He was beating
the shit out of Kandi."

"I knew something like this would happen,
didn't think he would disrespect me though, but
he will have to answer. Where were you at?"

"Right in front of here."

"Why didn't you holler for me?"

"I did, but you were too lost in some pussy
to hear me screaming at the top of my lungs."

"Watch your damn mouth, before your ass
catch another ass whooping."

I smacked my lips and rolled my eyes, "Moe do
you think you can take me home?"

"Yeah, let's roll."

"Nah, he can't. I didn't say he could. You
didn't ask me, now go get your funky ass in my
truck I'm gone take you home."

I limped out of the motel and climbed in the
backseat of his truck to wait for them to come
out. It took him five minutes to come out with
his sidekick right by his side. Honey was a
Spanish chick that thought she had her teeth
sunk into Blaque. It was something about
Honey, I just didn't like. Most thought it was
because of Blaque, he wasn't my man and half

of the time I couldn't stand him, it was just something about her that rubbed me the wrong way. As always Blaque got into the car bitching and I didn't want to hear it. Turning my head towards traffic I tuned him out hoping he would just play the music the rest of the ride. We came to a stop, at a red light. I turned my head the opposite way and the red truck stood out like a sore thumb. There Erica stood, outside the car busy talking on a cell phone. Before I could even think, I jumped out Blaque's truck and ran full force towards Erica. I didn't know where I got the courage to, but I tackled Erica like I was linebacker trying to win the super bowl. I could hear Blaque screaming my name; I knew I would catch a beating for this. But the ass whooping I had planned for Erica would make mine worth it, I thought.

"Your man wants to beat on me, well let's see how he feels about this bitch," I said throwing wild punches to Erica's body. The many years of physical and mental abuse flashed before my eyes forcing me to swing harder and faster. Making sure she felt every blow. I punched and punched on her balled up body until I felt hands on me, pulling me off.

"Bitch are you stupid, let's fuckin' go before someone calls the police." It was Blaque, his strong arms forcing me off Erica.

"THIS NOT OVER BITCH" I yelled as Blaque carried me back to the car. I locked eyes with Starr, "I'm coming for you to hoe." Just as Blaque threw me into the truck I caught a glimpse of Big, picking Erica up off the concrete I could see the blood that poured from her face. I shot daggers their way, it wasn't over, and more blood would be shed. At that point I was content with that, we all couldn't walk on the same earth.

"What the fuck is your problem Kandi? Bitch I'm not trying to go to war with that old head right now. Try some shit like that again bitch, you gone be the one left bleeding." Blaque rants fell on deaf ears.

At that point, I didn't give a fuck what he was saying, my adrenaline was pumping. He wasn't ready for war, but I was, and I plan on being the one coming out of it in one piece.

Blaque bitched all the way to the house, I was happy to see the house so I could stop listening to him bitch about nothing.

"Since your black ass wants to start fights, your ass working a double be ready with the other girls tonight."

"Yeah okay," I said rushing out the car and into the house. Once again my body had taken some blows, I ran a hot bath and used some Epsom salt to try and soothe my aches. It would only be a few more hours before I would be back on the blade.

My phone went off indicating a message. I grabbed my phone off the counter and headed back into the room, Redd wasn't home so I had the room to myself.

It was Moe, "*Hey little Mama, I hope you good. Just checking on you. It's been a rough week for you, I'm here if you ever wanted to talk."* I couldn't contain the smile on my face. Moe was forbidden, but he was so kind and genuine not like the other men who came and went in my life. He seems real not like Ice, who pretended to care for me. But Moe was a man and I knew just like the rest, he had another side.

Chapter 13

As much as I just wanted to lay in bed, I knew Blaque wouldn't have it. I wasn't ready to take another beating either, so I quickly dressed and waited for him to pull up. I prayed the night was easy and went fast, I was sore. Redd had the music blasting in the room as she danced around getting ready.

"Kandiland, you working a double today?"

"Yeah, it's my punishment."

"Damn you must be bringing in bank, he got you pulling a double."

"I make enough. I wish I didn't have to go, but you know him. When he says do it, we do it.

"Yeah, you on the Blvd tonight?"

"Yeah I'm gone work the Blvd, I have regulars I'm gone call when we get there."

"Well Blaque should be here any minute," Redd said walking into the restroom to finish putting on her make up. I laid back down and waited.

Blaque entered the house making his presence known with his secret call. "If you supposed to be on duty, your ass better be ready or I'm docking a hundred from your weekly pay, let's go." He walked back out, Redd and me grabbed our bags and dashed out the house.

Blaque dropped Redd, Honey, and I on the Blvd and was off to do other drop offs and pick up's.

"Hit Moe if any trouble surface," Blaque said before pulling off.

"Okay." We said in unison making our way towards the shopping center. It wasn't too busy which was fine with me. I hadn't seen Bam and Ecstasy in a while. I spotted them on the side of the building. I made my way towards them. I stopped when I saw Toni, a small time drug pusher. I waited until Toni walked off to walk up on the girls.

"What's good?"

"Hey, hey Kandiland." Bam said trying to hide the powder, she had just purchased from Toni.

"You know you my girls, I'm not here to judge you," I said to them. I know most women abused drugs to cope with the pain of being out here. Some wanted to escape the harsh reality that this had become their lives.

"So how y'all been?"

"I'm good Kandiland," Ecstasy said fidgeting with her fingers.

"How you doing Kandiland? How is it with that nigga Blaque?" asked Bam.

"It's cool, nothing to really brag about, why you acting funny E?"

"We heard what happened between you and Big, we were told to fuck you up on sight then call them and let them know. But you already know Kandiland, we fuck with you the long way. So you don't have to worry about that, but watch out for that bitch Starr, she has a chip on her shoulder and got it bad for you."

"Thanks Bam, I don't want y'all to get in trouble so I'm gone keep my distance. But I'm gone be waiting for that bitch Starr."

"You know it's all love this way Kandiland. Keep ya head up. You always know where to find us."

"I know!" I walked off leaving the ladies to handle their business. I couldn't believe Big; he couldn't do the job fully, so he put word to the girls to jump me. I made my way to the street to see if I could catch a date. Just as soon as my feet hit the concrete an all white Cadillac pulled up.

"What's ya name Suga?"

"It damn sure isn't Suga," I said to him. He was an older black man.

"Well what's your name?"

"Why? You the Police?"

"Nah, I'm no Pig." I could see him going into his pocket. He pulled out five twenty dollar bills. "Will this let me get your name?"

"What you want?"

"What can you do?"

I grabbed the handle of his door, I stopped and scanned the inside of his car before I got in.

"Touch me!"

Nisha Lanae

"What?"

"Touch me, so I know you're not the police."

"I told you Suga, I'm no Pig" he said running his hands up my thigh. "Damn, your skin so soft. Where too?"

"Go to the stop sign make a left, then a right. Back into the parking space at the apartments on your left hand side." I said watching him as he pulled off. I usually didn't mess with the black men, I wasn't racist but their stamina was too high, but he was old he couldn't last that long. It didn't take long for us to get to the abandoned apartment complex.

"So what you want?"

"What can my money get?"

"A little head and a quickie, five minutes tops."

"Five minutes, that's not enough."

"Of what I got it is, bet I have you cumin in three."

"I like that, let's start off with some head then."

"Cool, but I need my money first."

"What? I'm gone pay you."

"Money first, then service." He handed me the five twenty dollar bills, I put the money into my bra. He let his seat back and adjusted himself, ready to be serviced. I leaned over the seat and slowly unzipped his slacks. I fished for his penis, but I couldn't feel it at first. Finally I found it, he was extra small. I looked closer and was shocked. "WHAT THE FUCK IS THAT?"

I yelled. His penis looked like it had been hacked off, and he had a virgin as well.

"Shut up Bitch, and give me all your money." He said with a strong grip on my hair and a three inch knife to my throat. The car was still on, thinking quick I used my hand to put the car in drive, using my other hand I sent a blow to his stomach and bit down on what was supposed to be his penis. He hollered out stepping on the gas sending the car crashing into the brick wall in front of us, I grabbed the knife and got out of dodge running towards the motel. I didn't look back to see if he gave chase, I just kept running until I made it to the motel parking lot. I knocked hard with my fist on the door to the room Blaque did his business in. I saw his car parked outside.

"Blaque! Blaque!" I yelled. He swung the door open.

"What's wrong Kandiland?"
I had to catch my breath before I was able to speak.

"This he-she or whatever it was just tried to rob me. "

"He, She?"

"Yeah, I don't know what kind of freaky shit he had going on but his penis was gone, like it had been hacked off and it had a pussy too." Blaque burst into laughter, I didn't see it funny. I was still trying to wrap my head around what exactly was the gender of the he/she actually was.

"You good Kandi?" asked Moe.

"I'm good now, just a little freaked out."

"She alive, she good" Blaque said. I rolled my eyes.

"I'm gon' go back to the blade" I said walking towards the door. Blaque still had a grin on his face and I wasn't really feeling it. I didn't even wait to see if he said anything I just walked out the door. As I was leaving Honey was walking in, she looked me up and down before going into the room.

"I can't stand that bitch," I said to myself. Just as I made it to the end of the parking lot I heard my name being called.

"Kandiland," it was Moe. I waited for him to catch up to me. Just as he got to me, Officer Tulsa pulled up.

"Well, well what do we have here?"

"Hello Officer, may I help you?"

"I'm talking to the young lady son, beat it." Moe stepped closer to me. "She is good, this is my lady. We are just enjoying the night breeze."

"She's nobody lady," Tulsa laughed eyeing me. "You don't know who I am, do you son?"

"Officer Tulsa, that's who he is." I said hoping Moe caught on fast.

"Oh the infamous Officer Tulsa, I heard a lot about you. Don't try anything you may later on regret."

"Are you threating an officer of the law son?"

"I don't know what you talking about Sir. I know this, you better not put your hands on her again, or I will personally serve your ass a dose of your own medicine."

Tulsa laughed. "Son I can kill you, and will get a pat on the back, or even a promotion so try me. While you on the other hand try it and will be put under a three by three cell. Kandiland you better tell this bitch boy who I am."

I didn't speak; I enjoyed seeing Moe talk down to Tulsa.

"She doesn't have to tell me anything. You just remember what I said, Officer."

"I will see you again son, and let's see if that mouth is as big as you portray it to be. Kandiland, Blaque know you out here holding another man's attention? I hope you got that money."

"That's none of your business, your job is to protect and serve and you can't do that holding up our time. So go get you some coffee and donuts and enjoy your night Officer." Moe said grabbing me by the hand we walked towards Moe's car. Tulsa looked on before he pulled off, I knew he was pissed and he would inflict some pain on me for being dissed by Moe.

"So that's the officer who gave you some of those bruises on your beautiful face?"

"Yeah that's him, Officer Tulsa."

We looked down the street when we heard a scream. It was Tulsa and a working girl I had seen around a few times. He had her pinned on his squad car slapping her around.

"So he just goes around messing with y'all ladies?"

"He is the Law, he does whatever he wants. He has his favorite girls to mess with."

"That shit has to stop. Y'all go through enough with the niggas y'all dealing with."

"I know," I said. I couldn't be around Moe. I was scared I would do something I shouldn't have, I was emotionally attracted to him.

"Let me get back to work, before Blaque comes out here. Honey can't hold his attention that long. I'm not trying to catch another beating."

"I feel you. Kandi, when is your Birthday?"

"Why?" I asked.

"Just wanted to know, I wanted to get you something."

"It's in two weeks." I said walking back towards the blade, I had to get away from him. He was a temptation.

I walked with a smile on my face. Moe always had that kind of effect on me. I made it back to the blade and it was live.

"Kandiland," Redd called out.

"What's good Redd?"

"Ole boy, the cop. He was over here looking for you. He told me to tell you your little friend can't save you."

"Fuck him, but thanks Redd."

"You welcome, you know when Blaque gone be around?"

"He over there at the motel."

"Cool, I will be back. If anyone come looking for me, tell them hit my cell."

I watched Redd walk off, she had adapted to the life so quickly, and she lived for it. Every morning she was up and ready.

"Okay." I said scanning the streets to see if Tulsa was creeping anywhere. When I didn't see him I got to work.

I didn't do too badly for a night I didn't want to be out there. I didn't even have to do a lot of work. It wasn't until the wee hours of the night when Blaque made his rounds picking us up and doing drop offs.

"Moe busy, so I'm gone be collecting tonight. Have your money ready when I come to your rooms. If your roomie has to have their money counted you step out until I say you can come back."

No one said anything, we just went with the flow of everything like always.

When Blaque got to our room I stepped out first, hoping Redd didn't try any extras with Blaque like always. I was surprised, she was in and out in a flash.

I walked into the room, Blaque was sitting on my bed waiting for me. I walked in throwing the money on the bed.

"Kandiland, you been doing real good out there except a few fuck up's, but I know yo' 18th birthday coming up. So I'm gone give you a little party to celebrate."

"I'm good, I don't want one."

"I didn't ask you that. Just get sexy and prepare to have some fun. I'm out, have a good night." Blaque said walking out the room.

"Ugh" I said under my breath. I ran me a hot bath, and lit the freshly twisted blunt and watched the red flames burn the brown paper as I inhaled the smoke.

Chapter 14

It was my birthday, I was 18 years old. I didn't feel whole, like every year before I had to count it as another year not spent with my brother, not celebrating together. The day always brought some bad memories to me. I wasn't really into celebrating this year either, but Blaque wasn't hearing it. He had a night planned at a club in Hollywood, I had never had a birthday party, and I was nervous and anxious all at the same time.

I sat in the bath tub and I had to think, today I made 18 years old. No high school diploma, my years were invested in the streets and the life of being a loyal hoe. I sat and had to ask myself if this was really the life I wanted to live for the rest of my life? Can I change? Am I too deep in? The questions swarmed around my head. I remember a conversation between Ice and I, he harshly told me I was tampered goods and no one would ever want me. Was I too used up to be someone wife, girlfriend, or mother? I sat there with tears threatening to fall from my eyes. I didn't choose this life, but I kept at it. My ringing phone stopped me right in the mist of me breaking down.

"Hey sexy, how are you?" I answered. It was Thomas, a regular of mine. He was an older man strung out on Viagra and black pussy.

"Hey Kandiland, what time do you want to meet me? I have a surprise for you."

"Meet me at our spot, in about two hours."

"Okay, see you soon. Can I get a taste of that sweet Kandi?"

"It all depends on what kind of surprise you have for me Big Daddy."

"You're going to love it."

"If that's the case, Kandiland gone make sure you leave with an extra big smile today."

"Yes! See you soon."

I hung the phone up with Thomas and quickly called Blaque. "Daddy, I need a ride to the blade one of my regulars has money waiting for me."

"I'm in traffic, I will send someone. What time you need to meet him?"

"In two hours."

"Cool," Blaque said hanging up in my face.

"Rude ass!" I said to myself, finishing up my bath and figuring out what I would wear for the day. The time seemed to fly, before I knew it an hour had passed.

Just as I finally found something to wear and slid into it, I saw Moe's name flash across my screen. My stomach fluttered.

"Hello," I answered trying not to sound like I had the cheesiest grin upon my face.

"Hey Kandi, I'm downstairs, you needed a ride somewhere?"

"Yeah I will be down in a second."
I looked my self over once more. I had on a pin stripe Maxi dress that showed off all of my curves, my hair was slicked into a messy bun on the top of my head. My lips were shiny with lip glass glaze over them.
I walked outside and my heart skipped a beat, it was something about Moe I couldn't shake. He drove my insides crazy. I took my time walking to his car, I hope he didn't notice.
"Happy Birthday Girl."

"Thanks Moe, how are you?"

"I'm good, how about you Miss I'm finally grown."
I smiled "Shit I been grown."

"Well now you finally legal, little lady."

"It don't feel no different, I have been doing everything already. It's just another day."
I hadn't shared with anyone about Kris, which was a weak spot for me. I didn't want anyone to use that against me.

"That may be true, but you legal now on paper. Not just in the mind and on the streets. But fuck all that where does the birthday girl want to go?"

"Can you take me to the Spot, on Atlantic?" I didn't bother looking at him, because I know he wouldn't like where he had to take me.

"What?"

"Moe, today is not the day, please don't judge me."

"I'm not judging you Kandi, I just don't understand how someone so young, and pretty, can be so deep in this lifestyle?"

"Moe, you will never understand, it's more than it looks like. So can we just leave it at that? I don't want to have to do this every time I see you."

"Well make me understand, because right now all I am hearing are excuses."

"It's a lot, I was born into this lifestyle; I didn't choose it. Let's just leave it at that." I spat back, I knew he meant well, at least I hoped, but I didn't feel the need to explain my life. I didn't care what others thought about my life, but with Moe it was different, so I wanted him to just back off.

"We will for now." With that he pulled out the drive way and into traffic. The ride was quiet, we didn't have much to say after that. Many people can say change and do this and that, when they aren't living the life you are, or carrying the burdens you have.
When we pulled up to the motel, I hurried and jumped out, not wanting to hear Moe ask anything else.

"Thanks for the ride," I said closing his door. Halfway to the room I heard Moe's voice call out my name, I turned around.

"Have a good day, see you later." He didn't smile, but I knew he wanted to. He was upset. I couldn't figure out why Moe cared so much, many women threw themselves at him. Why he so vexed on me, was what I couldn't understand. I had to smile as he pulled off.

I rushed into the room, I still had an ample amount of time before Thomas would arrive. Thomas was into role playing, I pulled out the different outfits. I was trying to determine who I would be for the day. I decided on the Naughty Doctor outfit, a long white coat and red lace panties and bra under with matching come fuck me pumps. Once I was all dolled up to perfection, I sat on the bed and waited for Thomas.

There was a slight knock at the door, followed by a single knock; then two. It was Thomas code to see if we had gotten our normal room for the week. I slowly strutted to the door, I slowly opened it with a wide grin plastered on my face.

"Good afternoon Mr. Thomas. What seems to bring you by today?"

"Hello Nurse Kandiland, I'm not feeling too well. I'm having some pains. I was wondering if you had time and could squeeze me in, to ease this pain.

"Well come in and take a seat, I will see what I can do to ease your pain. Let Ms. Kandiland work her magic.

Thomas sat the bag he had in his hand down on the side of the bed, then took a seat on the shabby bed.

"So what's the issue that brings you to Nurse Kandiland today?"

"Just some pains," he said using his eyes to roam over my body.

"Okay, where is the source of your pain?"

"This is quite embarrassing, but I'm having some pains down stairs."

"Downstairs?" I asked looking at him, making sure if I heard him correct.

"Yeah" Thomas said shifting his eyes down to his penis. "Downstairs."

"Oh okay, down those stairs" I smiled a shy grin, knowing he loved when I played innocent.

"Well, let's get you out those pants so I can take a look."

Thomas stood to his feet, eagerly yanking his pants down. His penis was slight erect and free of any hair. He didn't have on any underwear, which was normal. I didn't ask Thomas, I didn't even try. As long as he had my money and came back every week, I was fine with his unusual tactics.

"Let me know when you feel any pains or discomfort."

"Okay."

I gently rubbed my hand up and down his penis, starting with the shaft and making my way to his tip.

"The pain is right there at the top" Thomas grunted, laying back some on the bed.

"Let me see if this will help" I said. Using the tip of my tongue, I licked around the head before easing just the tip inside my mouth; I lightly applied pressure on it.

"How does that make it feel?" I asked him, I saw the perplexed look on his face, and I knew he was enjoying it.

"Do that again, I don't think it was enough for me to be able to tell."

I slid him back into my mouth, this time I was gentle, using my muscles I squeezed as tight as I could using a little teeth.

"Oh shit," he grunted.

"How is that?"

"It's wonderful, the pain is slightly going away. I think more of that will take the pain away for some time."

I eased him back into my mouth, lapping my tongue up and down his penis creating a wad of saliva in my mouth. I spat the salvia on his penis and watched it sliding down, catching it before it dropped. Licking it all up I went back to working my magic on his penis. Thomas, and every other man I serviced love sloppy head; the sloppier the better.

"Yeah that's amazing, you little dirty whore" Thomas grunted, yanking my head up and down, pushing himself into my mouth.

I knew he was ready for me. I stood to my feet, pushing him back onto the bed. "You ready to slide into something wet?"

"Yes!" He grinned like a fat kid at an all you can eat buffet. I slid out of my panties and bra, leaving my heels and the coat on. I slid a new condom onto Thomas erect penis, climbing onto the bed, I straddled him. I slid on to his manhood, adjusted my hand around his neck, and started to wind my hips slow. I started to wind fast, the faster I winded my hips, the tighter I squeezed Thomas neck. My grip was so tight, Thomas eyes began to bulge and within seconds he was cumin'.

"Ugh!" He grunted gripping my butt checks, and took my breast into his mouth, humping inside of me as he released his entire hot load. I let Thomas finish, then I made my way to the bathroom to wash up and put the clothes that I came in, back on.

"Thanks for meeting me, on such short notice Kandiland."

"No problem, you know you're one of my favorites Thomas." It was the truth, Thomas worked in the Auto Mechanic business; he owned several of his own franchise businesses. He was one of my best tricks; he paid the most, and was the easiest to please. Thomas paid me twelve hundred dollars a week for two hours of my time. Thomas was recently divorced; his ex-wife was crazy and drove him insane, he had one daughter, she was deep into drugs and sucking him dry with rehab programs.

"Here is your gift." Thomas handed me the bag; he sat on the side of the bed, when he first came into the room.

"Thanks!" I took the bag from him and took out its contents. It was a set of diamond earrings with a matching necklace.

"Oh my goodness Thomas, this looks expensive, I can't take this."

"Yes you can, and you will. That's a small token of my appreciation. You give me the best sexual experiences I've ever had. You deserve it, every women deserves a nice gift from Tiffany's."

"Oh God, thanks Thomas!" I was in shock that he had given me such an expensive item.

"Happy birthday Kandiland, don't be out on these streets too long tonight. Enjoy yourself, I will see you next week."

"Okay, I will and thanks again Thomas, I love it."

Thomas had walked out the door, I was still stuck looking at the sparkly earrings and necklace.

I sent Blaque a text message and gathered my things, I hope he came for me and not Moe; I couldn't deal with his questioning anymore today.

Blaque didn't respond to my text, but I knew it was him outside laying on the horn. I slid two hundred dollars from the money Thomas gave me, sliding it into my secret stash and the rest into my purse pocket; I grabbed my bag and made my way outside. I jumped into the car, Honey and Redd was already inside.

"Moe running a little behind, so hold on to y'all money and he will swing by within the hour to collect."

We pulled up to the house, Honey stayed in another house elsewhere.

"Kandiland," Blaque called out right before I closed the door.

"Yeah."

"The bag on the floor, it's yours. Happy Birthday, it's your outfit for the night."

Honey was in the front seat, she smacked her lips and whispered something under her breath.

"Honey, say what you gotta' say out loud bitch!"

"We not about to start this shit today," Blaque yelled.

"Whatever," I said grabbing the bag. "Thanks Blaque." I made my way up the drive way, something told me to look back. My eyes met Honey's and the deadly glare she gave me.

"Bitch" I said to her, as Blaque pulled off. Honey and I just didn't see eye to eye, it was a mutual dislike we had for each other.

I made my way into the house to see what Blaque had bought me to wear for the night.

Chapter 15

The music was blaring as we stepped into the crowded club, being escorted into an exclusive area, meant for only us. I couldn't lie, I felt like royalty. The clubs décor was top of the line and from the looks of it, the owner held no expense. The waitress came to the table taking our orders; I hadn't had a drink in so long, I couldn't wait to feel the warm sensation go down my throat and the light burn in my chest.

The DJ was spinning all of the latest jams, I took a few shots that the waitress had left on the table and prepared myself for a great night.

I was winding my hips to the beat of Ciara's new joint. Blaque was somewhere in the crowd with a flock of women surrounding him.

"May I get this dance, Kandiland is it?" It was a tall guy, with dreads dressed in the latest fashions.

"How do you know me?" I asked nervously. I didn't introduce myself as Kandiland unless I was on the blade, the DJ introduced me as Kandi, when he mentioned my name over the mic.

"Your name is on the back of your vest," he smiled. "It doesn't take a rocket scientist to figure out that had to be your name."
I felt stupid, I had forgotten about the custom vest Blaque had gotten me to wear for the night. Kandiland was stoned in diamonds and spikes.

"I totally forgot about that, this was a gift," I said trying to cover up that I was slightly nervous.

"May I have this dance?"

"Sure" I replied. He grabbed my hand, leading to the crowded dance floor.
The DJ was spinning all the latest cuts, I hadn't noticed that we had danced for the last five songs, my feet were hurting and I needed something to drink.

"Thanks for the dance, have a great night."

"Aww, you done, this my jam; one more dance," the man plead.

"Sorry, I'm tired" I said to him making my way across the dance floor, back to our reserved area. Just as I took a seat to catch my breath, I felt a strong pair of hands tightly gripping the back of my neck.

"Bitch, don't you ever disrespect me like that again. If that nigga isn't paying you, you don't fuckin' entertain them."

"It was just a dance. Isn't that what people do in a club?" I asked, struggling to breathe, he applied more pressure on to my neck.

"Bitch you do as I say, you belong to me. There isn't shit you do, that is free unless you sucking' my dick. So don't let the shit happen again Kandiland, I'm not one of them hoes on the blade; so watch yo' fuckin' mouth."

"Yes" I replied quickly, hoping he would release the tight grip, he had on the back of my neck.

"What's good birthday girl?" Moe asked, walking up, breaking the tension between Blaque and me.

"It's good, just trying to have some fun and enjoy myself" I replied.

"This shit fly big bro" Moe said glancing around the club. "You gave little mama a big celebration."

"She kinda' deserved it, she keep acting an ass, she gon' pay for the money I dished out" Blaque said finally releasing my neck. I wanted to let him have it, but it wasn't the place. I knew he wouldn't hesitate to put a beating on me in the crowded club.

"Chill big bro, we all out here tonight trying to have a great time." Moe said shaking Blaque by the shoulders. "C'mon Kandi, let me see what you working with on the dance floor."
I looked at Blaque then to Moe, hoping Moe would read between the lines.

"I know big bro isn't trippin' about me and the birthday girl having a dance?" Moe asked really not caring what Blaque would say.
"C'mon Kandi."

I looked at Blaque, I knew Moe didn't care, I did. I wasn't trying to take another slap to the face today.

"Don't be getting my little bro dick hard and shit," Blaque said.

Moe didn't waste any time lingering around for Blaque to protest, he grabbed my hand and lead me to the dance floor, just as my favorite joint by E-40 and Too Short came on.

I started to rock my hips to the beat of the song; Moe grabbed me by my hips and rocked with me to the beat, as I shook my goodies on him. I could feel the temperature rise; Moe was a bit tipsy and began to get hard. I could feel his manhood rising through the short spandex shorts I had on. Moe's hands began to slide from my hips to my thighs then in between my legs. I knew we were playing with fire, but it was Moe, and I liked the feeling he was giving me. I looked around for Blaque; I knew he would be watching us, clocking our every move.

When I looked up I noticed Blaque was pre-occupied with company. I grabbed Moe by the hand and practically dragged him off the dance floor into a dark corner.

"Where in the hell are we going?"

I didn't respond. I pinned Moe against the wall, letting my lips lay on his. Moe gripped me by my butt, pulling me closer to him; letting our lips intertwine. Moe used one hand to reach over and caress my swollen vagina lips, I couldn't lie, the feeling felt amazing. I couldn't help but let a soft moan escape my mouth, at that point I didn't care who was watching.

I wanted to please Moe, he always looked out for me, and I wanted to make him feel good. I dropped to my knees playing tussle with his pants and belt.

"Whoa, Kandi you don't have to do this." Moe said gripping my arm, trying to lift me from the ground. But it was too late, I had already freed his harden member and had him in the contours of my mouth. I slurped up and down Moe's manhood until he erupted in my mouth.

Moe laughed while fixing his pants. "Kandi, you wild ass shit, you gon' fuck around and get us killed" he laughed again. "Let's get back on this dance floor before they come looking for us."

We made our way back to the dance floor, bumping into Honey on our way. She glared at us, turning her nose up and whisking off. We paid her no mind, we partied the night away. The DJ announced last call for alcohol; I took three more shots of patron to the head.

I walked out the club on cloud nine, without a care in the world. It was the first time I had ever celebrated my birthday, and it was amazing. I hadn't noticed Blaque approaching or the look on his face. All I felt was a burning sensation to my face, and the taste of blood. Blaque had smacked the fire from me, causing my lip to bust.

"Bitch, I don't care if it's your birthday. I keep telling you not to fuckin' disrespect me."

"What the fuck is going on?" Moe asked, running up from behind us.

"This bitch keep disrespecting me."

"What she do?" Moe asked, trying to stand in front of Blaque so he wouldn't strike me again.

"Mind yo' business nigga, and let me handle mine. That bitch my business," Blaque sneered maliciously. He had me pinned against the wall, his hand wrapped tightly around my neck.

"Bro, we in a public place you faded, this isn't the time nor place."

"Fuck you little nigga, I'm your older brother. Stay in yo' fuckin' lane nigga, you want to fuck my bitch nigga? Huh? You want to fuck this hoe?"

"Blaque, you faded and talking real fuckin' reckless tonight, just get into the car and handle this shit later." Moe was beginning to become agitated with Blaque and his drunken rants.

"Nah, fuck that. Honey told me how you and this bitch were dry fucking on the dance floor, and went to the back." Blaque spat, his eyes screamed danger as he looked between Moe and I for answers.

"Where Honey at? Since she wants to tell lies."

Moe stormed to the bus in search of Honey. Moe dragged Honey from the bus.

"Now what's this shit you feeding my brother that has him all fired up?"

"I told him I saw you and Kandi," she pointed to me. "On the dance floor, all close and grinding on each other, then y'all went somewhere together." Honey smirked.

"We were dancing, it's a club. That's how dancing goes, but that other shit you fuckin' lying. We were on the dance floor, the whole time."

"Nigga, why you lying? I saw y'all. You and Kandi were in the little corner together" Honey yelled trying to defend herself.

"Blaque you know damn well, that Honey doesn't like Kandi. Hell everyone out here knows that. Tonight Kandi had a lavish birthday party, thrown by you. Can you see why Honey throwing shade?" I knew Moe was trying to save me; he was throwing all the cards out, but he was telling the truth, Honey hated me. She always threw shade my way, even though she standing there telling the truth, I wasn't going to give her the satisfaction of seeing me take a beating. I was so grateful for Moe at that moment.

"Honey, bitch are you lying on my brother?" Blaque, let his grip on my neck go to focus on Honey.

"No Daddy, I know what I saw. Why would I stand here and lie to you?"

"What your messy ass saw, was two people having a friendly dance. You just tryna' start something, because tonight wasn't about you, and you hated that shit. Now you out here tryna' start some shit between me and my blood, that's

154

my brother, remember that. You messy rotten pussy bitch," Moe spat.

Blaque stood glaring at all of us, he didn't know who was lying and who was telling the truth.

"Daddy, you just gon' let him talk to me like that?"

Blaque didn't say anything. We just stood there not knowing what to expect. Blaque smacked Honey viciously, sending her flying to the ground.

"You better never lie on my family again, you better not even speak ill of him or I will kill you bitch. Bro drop these bitches off. I'm gon' send for a car, I'm tired of looking at these bitches. I'm about to go lay up in some new pussy."

"Do you bro, I'm at you later." Moe got us all back into the bus, Honey shot daggers at us the whole ride.

Moe allowed the bus driver to drop everyone off at their houses. Redd and the rest of the ladies in my house, were still on the blade. Moe left me for last, we got dropped off to his car.

"Thank you or standing up for me."

"You good little mama, how is your face and lip?"

"It's cool, I've had worst done, I will survive."

"Yeah you will, but that shit isn't cool."

"It comes with the life I live, I'm used to it."

"That's some shit, you shouldn't be getting use to little mama," Moe said glancing my way.

I knew he meant well, but I wasn't in for it tonight.

"Can we not do this tonight Moe?" I said. He didn't respond, but I could see him clinching his jaws, he was mad. My head was spinning; I didn't have time to go back and forth with Moe about my life.

Traffic was non-existent at this time of the morning, Moe zoomed in and out of lanes. I closed my eyes and let the cool breeze soothe me. The car came to a stop, I heard Moe's door open and close. The smell of fishy water, tickled my nose. I opened my eyes and we were parked at the beach. Moe took a blanket from the trunk of his car and laid it on the sand. I removed my shoes and went to join him.

"Whenever I'm going through something, I come to the beach late at night. Just to think and clear my mind, the water helps me relax," Moe said glazing out at the water.

"It's so peaceful out here."

"I know, when my grandmother passed I came here with everything to unwind; and to just get away from all the bullshit."

"I'm sorry to hear that." I said to him, it made me think. I never knew what it felt like to have grandparents. I didn't know anything about Big's family, and Madam didn't have any.

"Each day, it gets easier to deal with, but the pain never goes away."

"Is that the only family Blaque and you had?" I questioned.

"Yeah, I never met my father, he was killed before my mother found out she was pregnant with me. When I was five, my mother was killed. She died from a concussion to her brain, from being in an abusive relationship with her drunk of a boyfriend."

I could hear the sadness in Moe's voice, he was hurting. I wrapped my arms around him trying to offer him whatever comfort I could, he always seemed to be there for me, it was the least I could do.

"We moved in with our grandmother after that. She stayed on us about school and our studies, wanted us to be better than my mom's and uncles. She always told me, I would make something of myself and do great things. Everyone knew Blaque wouldn't amount to much, since he was young, he was always rebellious and loved inflicting pain on others."

"How did your grandmother pass, if you don't mind me asking?"

"They said a heart attack, she was scared to death. Some men showed up to our house looking for Blaque. He had gotten into it with some dudes who he shorted for twenty g's. They came demanding the money from my grandmother, Blaque was out of town. She passed out. They left her there, when I got home, it was too late. She had already died." A single tear slid down his face, as he spoke. I knew he was hurting.

"That was three years ago, I never really forgave Blaque for it, his wrong doings caused her death in my eyes. My grandmother was my heart; I know she is smiling down on me, at the man I am becoming."

"So why do you still hang around Blaque so much?" I questioned.

"He is my brother, the only real family that I have left. I know he has some fucked up ways, but I know my grandmother wouldn't want me to just turn my back on him. She didn't raise us to be that way. I try to hold onto him, as much as I can; hoping one day he will change."

"Damn, do you know why he chose to get into pimpin'?"

"It's in his blood, from my understanding our pops was a pimp and so was his father."

"Your mother was a ......"

Moe just looked at me cutting off my sentence. "I gave you my story, so what's yours Kandi? How did you get out here? I know my brother he has a gift of gab, I've seen him talk a women out of her panties."

"I'm the product of a Pimp and Madam; this is the life I was born into. My father is a pimp and my mother was his main hoe. Since me and my brother were conceived, my parents molded us for this lifestyle, to be the next generation of what they call the family enterprise."

"You have a brother?"

"Yeah a twin brother."

"Where is he? If you don't mind me asking."

"I don't know, I haven't seen him; since our fifteenth birthday. My mother put me out at 15,

when she caught her husband and me fucking."
It wasn't until that moment that I felt a slight
pain, for the life I was dealt. Just as the tears
was about to fall, I sucked them back up. I
didn't want a pity party, it was the cards I was
dealt, so I had to play the hand the very best that
I knew how.

"It's okay to cry Kandi, I'm not here to
judge you, you don't always have to bottle your
inner feelings in, and you don't always have to
be tough." Moe said, his voice pledging with
me.

"I'm solid, its life, there is no need to cry." I
replied, staring off into the water.
Moe grabbed my chin, until my eyes locked
with his. "Your mouth is telling me that, but
your eyes are telling me something else."
I couldn't hold back the tears anymore, a river
of tears cascaded down my face. Moe gently
wiped my face.

"Let's get you home, tonight has been crazy
for you." Moe lifted me off my feet, grabbing
the blanket; he carried me off to his car.
The ride to the house was silent, I could tell
Moe was condemned to his own personal
thoughts, from the corner of my eyes I watched
him. We pulled up to the house, Moe killed the
engine, and he didn't say a word. I started to
grab my things; I was tired and ready to get
some rest.

"Hold up, I'm gon' come inside and wait for
the girls to hit me."

"Okay." I waited for Moe to get out the car, and followed behind him inside.

"I'm gon' take a quick shower, the remote is on the nightstand."

"Cool."

I went into the bathroom and washed away the nights sweat and stress. I put lotion on my body and slid into the oversized t-shirt and joined Moe back in my room. He was sprawled out on my bed.

"I don't bite, you can come lay next to me," Moe laughed. "You can change the channel to whatever you want to watch." He said handling the remote to me.

"Nah, this is fine. I love watching the re-runs of Fresh Prince of Bel-Air and Martin." I replied laying down next to him, the smell of his cologne and sweat mixed, clogged my nose.

"Me too, Martin and Will funny ass shit, in their younger days."

"Yeah, they were."

We sat and watched the re-runs laughing and joking. It was simply fun, and felt great.

"Do you ever want to get married? Or have kids?" Moe asked.

"I've never really gave it a thought, how about you?"

"I've always wanted a wife and some kids, the whole white picket fence life."

"I don't think I'm the wife type of girl."

"Why do you say that?" Moe questioned sitting up, staring at me."

"I don't know what it takes to be a girlfriend, I tried it once, and that didn't work well. Ice, fucked over me just like every other man."

"Not all men are the same, you can't judge all men on the fucked up men that came through your life. There is someone for everyone."

"So why are you single Moe, you're a handsome guy and have a lot going on for yourself, why don't you have a woman?"

"The right one hasn't come along; there are plenty of women that throw themselves at me daily. I want someone that would make my moms and grandmother proud, a woman I know they would have approved of."

"They meant a lot to you?"

"Yeah, those women meant the world to me."

"I hope you find that woman, you deserve her Moe, you're a good guy."

"Sometimes that person can be in your face, and you never know it, because you don't realize it."

"Well, I hope she realizes it."

"I hope so too" he smiled. "Let me go check on these girls, it's getting late."

"Okay, thanks Moe, for everything."

"You can show me, by giving me a nice big hug," Moe laughed.

I jumped into Moe's arms wrapping my arms around his neck. He squeezed me into his arms, his breath tickled my neck, causing my heart to beat fast. Moe lightly sucked my skin into his mouth planting passionate kisses on my neck and collar bone. My nipples hardened under the thin oversized shirt, my kitten began to purr. Our lips locked, doing a dance to our heart beats, Moe sat on the bed, pulling me into his lap. His hands slid underneath my shirt caressing on my body. Moe slid my shirt over my head, taking my harden nipple into his mouth.

Moe laid me on the bed, looking me deep in my eyes. "Tonight Kandi, I want to please you. You don't always have to please a man, sometimes you need to be pleased. I want to give you that." Moe spread my legs, planting tender kisses on my freshly waxed kitten. I hadn't experience oral pleasure since Ice, it was a no-no in the life, and you only were able to give head, never receive it. Moe was skillful with his tongue; he explored every part of my kitten sending an electric volt through my body. Moe tongue fucked me until my legs started shaking; I whaled out in pleasure, experiencing the best orgasm that I ever had in my life.

Moe stood up, dropping his pants to the floor, his erect manhood sprung out. My kitten was begging for him to scratch the itch that I had. Moe let his tongue find its way down my throat, as he eased into my moist opening. Moe slowly stroked inside of me, he was bigger than any man I had ever been with. I laid there lost in the bliss of me and Moe's sexual experience. He took his time kissing, nibbling and sucking on my body. I knew it was kind of cliché, but for the first time, I felt like I was being made love to. I felt my body twitching, I knew another orgasm was coming along; it was the third one of the night. Moe was reaching his eruption; I felt the way his body tensed up. He moved slowly, gripping my chin, forcing my eyes to lock with his.

"Kandi, I don't just want your body or your mind. That's what you gave Ice, my brother and your father. I want what you haven't given to any other man, I want your heart."

His words felt like sweet melody to my ears, but I lived in reality. I couldn't be the woman he needed in life, the woman made for him. What Moe wanted, I didn't have to give.

Moe kissed my lips, his phone had been going off for the last hour. Moe quickly got dressed.

"I will see you later little mama." Moe said kissing my lips again, before heading out the door. I laid in my bed, naked; replaying what just took place in my head. I gathered myself together; I knew soon the girls would be filling

into the house. I changed my sheets, showered and sprayed the room, before falling fast asleep.

Pounding The Pavement

Chapter 16

It had been weeks since my birthday party,
and the Players Ball was coming up. Blaque was
so pre-occupied with getting things in order for
his big night that he hadn't paid much attention
to me and Moe developing relationship. Since
my birthday every other day, we met at the
Spot. I knew if we ever got caught, Blaque
would kill us for our betrayal.
Just like any other day, I spent time with Moe.
Then made my way back to the blade. Making
sure not to go unnoticed for a while, so no one
can say they hadn't saw me. I took the back
streets, passing Lueders Park; I could see the
crowd of gang members hanging out and a few
squad cars, parked alongside the curb, harassing
people as usual. I noticed Tulsa's squad car
parked. I made sure to not pass them, and
headed down another side street. I hadn't saw
him in weeks, there was a lot of gang killings in

the area lately, so he didn't have much time to spare chasing working girls on the blade.

I could hear a car approaching from behind, something in my heart told me it was Tulsa. I glanced back and sure enough it was. *"Fuck"* I thought to myself. I knew if I ran, he would give chase and make whatever he had planned for me even worst for me.

"What Tulsa?"

"You been dodging me Kandiland? I haven't been able to get my dick wet lately. You know that doesn't make me happy."

"Tulsa, how many other working girls are you fuckin' without paying? I'm sure one of them could get your dick wet."

Officer Tulsa jumped out his squad car, pinning me up against the brick wall in the alley. "I don't want those other bitches, I want yo' ass, I've told you before about checking in."

"Tulsa, you don't own me, I don't have to check in with you, you don't even pay me."

"Bitch I'm the fuckin' police, I run fuckin' Compton and all of you funky hoes. Now open the fuck up and let me get my nut in."

"Fuck you, you fat fuck. You might as well take it like you always do; because I'm not willingly giving you any pussy" I spat. I was fed up with Tulsa; I knew my mouth would get me a beating. At that moment I didn't care, I was tired of his abuse, fuckin' me when he wanted and not paying me a dime. Tulsa took advantage of me, just as he was about to deliver a blow to

my face. An emergency call about a shooting in
the area came through dispatch.

"You better be glad, I have to take this; I
will catch up to you later."

"Whatever I hope one of them bloods, fuck
your ass up; you fuckin' cracker." I yelled at his
squad car as he zoomed down the alley.
I rushed back toward the Spot, I had left my bag
of changing clothes and feminine products
inside the room. Moe's car wasn't in the parking
lot anymore, but Blaque's was. I knew I
couldn't be seen, he would wonder why my bag
was left inside. We didn't use these rooms for
tricks, just for handling money and hide outs. I
stood outside trying to figure out what I would
say.
I watched as Blaque storm out the room and
jump into his car.
I ducked down as he sped out of the driveway.
He looked baffled by something, passing
without ever noticing me. I crept back into the
room, quickly cleaning myself up, and making
my way back to the blade.
I saw Redd ducked in the cut, staying away
from the traffic; the police were still patrolling
like crazy, because of the double homicides not
to far from the blade.

"Kandiland," Redd called out. I met her in
the cut, between the two buildings.

"What's good Redd?"

"Blaque was around looking for you, people
been saying they haven't seen you in hours. The
police sweating Blaque tough."

167

"Why?" I asked.

"I'm not sure he just said for you to hit him."

"Cool, I will. Thanks Redd."

I was hungry, so I made my way into the Chinese food place to get something to eat. Blaque's truck pulled alongside me, as I made my way through the parking lot.

"Get in" Blaque said.

I jumped into the car's front seat, no one else was in the car, and his gun was sitting on his lap. I became nervous, I hardly saw him driving around with his gun exposed.

"What's good?"

"Who you been talking to Kandiland?"

"What you mean, who I've been talking to?"

"The police have been on me all day, who you talking to? You telling ya' little fat white pig trick my business?"

"You trippin' what the fuck I look like, I'm not dumb. Why would I tell him anything, I can't stand his ass? There's been several killings around here, you are known, maybe the police just seeing if you had anything to do with it. You know the police don't like you, you're a known gang member, drug dealer and pimp."

Blaque sat and rationalized what I had said to him. "When the last time you saw Tulsa?"

"Earlier, when I was coming from the spot."

"The spot?" Blaque asked looking at me.

"I was on a date, we parked in the back of the lot, I was walking past the alley, when he pinned me up and you know the rest."

"So you still fuckin' him without pay?"

168

"I wouldn't call that fuckin' and what you want me to do about the money, he not giving me shit. I thought that was a part of your job? To handle him."

"Don't worry I will handle Tulsa soon, you just keep bringing in my fuckin' money."

"I hope sooner than soon, I'm tired of that motherfucka' raping me."

"Like I said, he gon' get handled, now get back to work. I will be back in a few hours." I jumped out the car and got to work, since spending time with Moe, I had to make extra money to cover up the fact for hours out the day; I was laid up with Moe, and not a paying trick.

Chapter 17

It was a lavish event planned, every year. These years the player's ball had changed from its original events in the past, the players of the game had changed, and so did the game.
It was mid- November and the leaves began to fall, it was my favorite season of the year. The weather wasn't too cold, or too hot. It was the biggest night of the underworld of sex; it was also the big birthday bash for Bishop Don Marcos. It was my very first year attending the lavish event that everyone talked about. Blaque only took his top money makers to the event with him, we were dressed to impress in long evening gowns.

It had been months since the incident with Big and Madam and I knew chances were I would see them tonight. I didn't know how I would act, being in their presence. I put it to the back of my mind, and focused on the event. I put my poker face on and prepared for a great night.

We pulled up in a cocaine white Mercedes Benz Limo, it felt like a red carpet event. Like something I watched on television, as we pulled up and walked down the pathway leading into the W Hotel, where the event was being held. Blaque was a gangsta and his stride and demeanor proved it in every sense, but the way he rocked the butterscotch tailor made tuxedo, crimson colored Stacy Adams, he demanded attention as he bypassed the others waiting to get in. Everything about him screamed boss, including me and Redd who stood on each of his arms. Our matching Versace gowns, hugged every hump and curve in our body.

We were escorted to our seats, you would have thought this was the awards. The lay out was gorgeous, something straight out of a magazine. There were cameras flashing everywhere, catching every moment.

As we took our seats, Madam's words popped into my head. *"Pussy has power, it can take you to some places outside of the hood; you would never know."*

I sat there, and believed her words. I never would have imagined, I would be standing in a room full of pimps and hoes, from all around the country for such a lavish event.

"This some fly shit Kandiland," Redd said sitting next to me.

"It sure in the hell is. I can get used to this life. I swear I can."

"Bitch for real, they got all kinds of food over there, and did you see they have Ace of Spade bottles everywhere. They went all out with this damn shit" Redd said in amazement.

Redd and I sat at the table talking, we were star struck, celebrities filled inside the Hotels ball room. I could feel eyes watching me. We were in a sea of sharks, the rules still applied, no direct eye contact with another pimp. Blaque was sitting there in a deep conversation with an attractive woman, not paying us any attention. It gave me a chance to scan the room. My eyes locked with the infamous Big, and his two sidekicks Madam and Starr. I didn't hold my glaze long, Big wasn't the exception, he still was a pimp. I got up and excused myself to the restroom.

I walked into the ladies room; it was empty minus the one person in the stall. I paced the floor, trying to gather my thoughts. I used the sink for leverage, holding my head down. I heard the door open; I didn't pay much attention to who entered.

I felt a hand run down my back. "Awe honey are you okay?" It was Madam, I hated her voice and it made my skin crawl. Flashbacks of my childhood and her cruel attitude flooded my vision.

"Get your fuckin' hands off of me," I said turning to face her.

"Now is that anyway to speak to your mother?" Madam asked with a slight grin plastered on her face.

"You are hardly a mother; the only thing you did was spit me out that funky pussy between your legs."

"Oh I did much more than that, I carried you and your brother for nine months and underwent 13 hours of labor, countless nights of getting no sleep, waking up in the middle of the night feeding you. You looking real good baby girl, body is in shape, skin is radiant. I always told you there was power in the pussy. I guess you learned to put that pussy to use," Madam chuckled.

"You get a kick out of this shit don't you?"

"I'm just saying; don't ever say I didn't teach you anything. Pussy is what got you where you are, and I taught you that, it was power in the pussy. So don't you ever forget that, you little ungrateful bitch."

"Some mother you are, what you want the best pussy trainer award. Huh? Is that what you want mommy dearest? What kind of mother teaches their daughter to fuck and suck a dick and how to be a great hoe?"

"You were breed to be, it was your destiny, I'm not shit and neither are you, get used to it."

"You may not be shit, but don't include me in that bullshit."

"You're my offspring Kandi, get use to it. Sex will be the only thing your good at. I taught you, to use what you already possessed."

"I'm nothing like you, stay the hell away from me."

"You think your better than me, but you're not. We are one in the same Kandi."

"Fuck you, we are not the same," I sneered. Madam just chuckled "you have a lot to learn about life, my dearest Kandi."
I didn't say anything, her voice and everything about her agitated me. "Give Big, this message for me." I lifted my hand and brought it down on the side of her face, sending her flying into the bathroom stall.
I walked out the ladies room. I had been gone too long, and hoped Blaque hadn't noticed.

"Kandi where the fuck you been?" Blaque asked as soon as I took a seat.

"I had to use the ladies room, it was crowded."

"Yeah okay, let me find out you talking to any of these niggas or they hoes."

I just smiled "I'm not going nowhere daddy."

I didn't speak on the little altercation between Madam and me because it wasn't Blaque's issues it was mine. In due time, I would be handling it according to how I saw fit.

The night was going great, even with the many stares and frowns we received. Redd and I just shook them off and smiled. There had been a series of performers, this one guy had caught my eyes, I couldn't make out all the details of his face, because I didn't want to be caught staring at another man. They introduced him as Money, he got onto the stage and instantly his voice commanded the audience attention. He looked familiar, I just couldn't place his face. I knew the voice, it sounded like a male version of mine. I closed my eyes to listen to the voice, it was him, I knew the voice and it had grown with a deeper base. It was Kris, my heart skipped a beat, I had to get closer to the stage, and I had to know if it was him. It had been three years since I had last saw him, he was taller, had facial hair, his voice much deeper. It was Kris, my twin brother.

"I need to see him, talk to him," I said to myself.

"What did you say Kandi?" Redd asked.

"Nothing, I was just saying he was dope."

"Hell yeah, and he sexy ass fuck. I love them   thug niggas," Redd beamed.

"Girl hush, before Blaque hears you and puts his foot up ya' ass."

"Girl, he not paying us no damn mind" Redd replied.

I looked over and sure enough, Blaque was engaged in a conversation with an older gentleman.

Money's showcase was over; he thanked everyone and ran off the stage. With my eyes I followed him. He stopped and talked to a woman, then went through a door and he was gone.

Redd was talking, but it fell on deaf ears, my mind was racing. I had to find Kris.

The night was winding down, awards had been given out. They were down to the last award, pimp of the year. Everyone was on the edge of their seat waiting to see whose name would be called. The M.C. ran off a series of names before announcing Blaque as the winner. He beamed with pride. He stood up, with me and Redd on his arms. His cocky stride, showed how arrogant he was. He loved the attention everyone was giving us. Blaque fed off of attention, things like that made his dick hard. Blaque accepted the award, giving a short speech, while we just stood and smiled. Blaque got a kick out of the envious stares he received as we made our way towards the exit to the waiting limo.

"Did y'all bring a change of clothes, like I told you?"

"Yeah we did," Redd replied.

"Good, we gon' stop and change, then head to this after hours spot for a little shindig, since I'm the peoples champ, the pimp of the year."

"Okay," we replied watching him suck the white substance into his nose.

"Redd c'mon over here and get you some of this candy, I know you want some like always." Blaque smiled, licking his lips.
Without saying a word Redd moved until she was in between Blaque's legs, sucking a line up her nose.

"Kandiland, c'mon over here and get you some candy."

"Nah, I'm good daddy. I got some weed in my bag," I replied. Drugs weren't my thing, I seen what it could do to people, weed was the only thing I indulged in.

"Bitch, did I ask you that? It wasn't a fuckin' option, it's a demand. I run this shit, now come get you some candy like I said."

"I'm good," I said again.
Blaque sat the small glass tray next to him, I knew what was coming next. "So you want to disrespect me, after I brought you to this lavish event and you gon' disrespect me?" Blaque

snatched me by the hair, dragging me onto the side of the limo where he sat.

"Now snort a line."

I grabbed the rolled up dollar bill, I snorted a line of the deadly substance. It was a slight tingly in my nose, causing it to run a little.

"Snort another line," Blaque demanded.

"Nah, I'm good."

POW! Blaque's hand rested on the side of my face. "Snort another line. What you think, you too damn good to sniff a little powder?"

"No daddy," I pleaded.

"I know you're not, because you sell pussy for a living. You not shit, and not gon' be shit. Get the fuck out my face. We dropping yo' funky ass off." Blaque spat, flinging me by my hair, onto the other side of the limo.

"Redd, come over here and give me some head my dick hard." Blaque said pulling his erect penis from his pants. Redd squatted in front of him, taking him into her mouth.

I sat across from them, blocking out the loud slurping sounds. I looked out the window. I needed to find Kris, I had too.

We pulled up to the motel and I gladly exited the limo, I wanted to get far away from Blaque.

"Kandiland you staying here until Moe come get ya' funky ass, Redd get ya' shit, we have somewhere to be."

Nisha Lanae

I changed my clothes and waited for Moe to pick me up. I felt funny, my body felt numb. I laid down hoping Moe didn't take too long to arrive.

"Kandi... Kandi!" I heard someone call, my head was spinning. I couldn't make out the figure, neither the voice. My heart raced, my throat was dry.

"Kandi, you okay?"
I felt hands on my body, it was hot. I felt cool water hit my skin.

"Kandi, what have you took?" It was Moe.

"He made me do it, he made me snort it" I cried. I was scared; I never felt my heart race like that before. Moe washed my body and changed my clothes.

"Let's get you something to eat" Moe said putting me into his car. Moe drove me to the house, it was empty all the girls were out working the blade.
It took hours, and Moe held me the whole time. I had finally started to feel like myself. My heart had stop racing and my body was no longer numb.

"Thanks for staying here with me Moe."

"You know that's never a problem. You scared me there girl, don't ever do that shit again."

"I scared myself, and you don't have to worry about that. Drugs aren't my thing, and tonight showed me they never will be. I didn't like how it made me feel."

"Good, now let me get out of here, will I see you tomorrow at the spot?"

"Yeah, but why wait for tomorrow on what can be done today?" I said pulling Moe by his waist towards me.

"What you up to girl?" Moe asked smiling. Putting his soft lips against mine letting his tongue explore mine. Redd wouldn't be in tonight, she never did when she left with Blaque. Moe wasn't due to pick up the other girls for another hour. He unbuckled his pants and let them fall to his knees, parted my knees like the red sea and he pleased my body.

Chapter 18

The weather had begun to decrease; it was raining more than ever. I didn't know if there was anything going around, but I wasn't feeling good; and hadn't been for the last two days. I couldn't hold anything down and my head was spinning.

"Kandiland, Blaque gon' be here in an hour to pick us up he said," Redd said to me.

"I'm not feeling good, tell him I'm gon' take the next shift. I need to rest right now."

"What's wrong?" she asked moving closer to my bed.

"I'm just not feeling good, I can't hold anything down." Just as the words left my mouth, I ran to the bathroom throwing up the few saltine crackers, I had eaten moments before. "Nothing is agreeing with my stomach."

"Okay I will let him know, I hope you feel better soon, if not you better get that checked out. You know Blaque not gon' allow you to lay on your ass for too long, he losing money."

"Yeah I know," I said climbing back into my bed. Throwing the covers over my head and falling asleep.

When I finally woke up, I had five missed calls from Blaque and a slay of unread text messages. I hit call back, calling him back.

"What's good daddy?"

"I hear you not feeling good, I'm gone be at the house in an hour so you can go to the doctor's office, Redd gone go with you."

"Okay."

I got up and made me a small bowl of oatmeal, hoping it would stick. I took a hot shower and threw on some sweats and a t-shirt and waited for Blaque to arrive. I didn't see why Redd had to tag along. She had been acting funny lately, I knew she had to offer her services to him.

I heard Blaque loud engine pull into the drive way. I grabbed my bag and headed out the door, Redd was in the front seat, I hopped in the back. We pulled up to the Long Beach Medical Center, Blaque let us out in the front.

"Hit me when y'all done."

"

Okay."

 Once I checked in, I decided to see where Redd head was, she had been distant and acting strange lately.

"Blaque said you told him I was throwing up, and had been feeling sick for a few days now?"

"I told him you was throwing up, and that you may have eaten something bad, and that I would sit with you at the doctors so you wouldn't have to wait alone." Redd said, her eyes were focused on her phone she never looked at me.

Just as she finished her sentence they called my name.

"I will be back."

"You don't want me to come with you?"

"Nah I'm a big girl, I can go by myself" I told her. Redd was the worst actress ever, I knew she was there for a reason.

I got to the back; it was so many people waiting in the halls. The doctor asked me a series of questions, taking my urine sample and blood work. They sent me back to the lobby to wait for the test to be ran. I got to the lobby, Redd was glued to her phone, there was someone holding up a lot of her time. She was smiling at the phone, never seeing me approach her.

"You over here just grinning, somebody must have a crush or something?"

"It's nothing like that, it's my cousin, she funny as shit" Redd said. She never looked me in my face. I knew she was lying.
It felt like we had been there for hours waiting for my name to be called.

"Miss. Timmons's" a young nurse called out.

"I will be back in a second Redd."
I followed the nurse towards the back, she escorted me to a room.

"The Doctor will be in shortly Miss." The young Hispanic nurse said, sitting my chart on the counter. I was nervous; I didn't know what was going on.
A small Indian woman entered the room. "Hello Miss Timmons's, I'm Dr. Ollie."

"Hello Doctor."

"Well we got your lab work back, and from the information on your screening. We estimate your about six weeks pregnant."
I felt weak. "What? This can't be right, please tell me that this is a joke?"

"No Miss Timmons's."

"Call me Kandi" I told her.

"Well Kandi, we ran the test through your urine sample and blood work. You are definitely pregnant. We can schedule an appointment for you at the women's clinic to discuss your choices." I heard Dr. Ollie talking, but everything had become a blur to me, I was confused. How could this happen to me.

I took the papers from Dr. Ollie and made my way back towards the lobby. I was stuck, and I didn't know what to do. Blaque couldn't find out, he couldn't have kids, which would give me and Moe up. I knew it wasn't Tulsa, I found out long ago all he shot were blanks, those were the only three, I engaged in sex with without protection.

I took a seat my mind racing a million miles an hour.

"You good Kandiland?" Redd asked.

"Yeah, my stomach still hurting, you were right. It was something I ate."

"You want me to call Blaque, and let him know you ready?"

"Yeah, tell him I'm ready" I was too lost in my own thoughts; I sat the papers on the small table beside me. I closed my eyes to prevent the tears from falling.

I had to get in touch with Moe, to get rid of this before Blaque found out. I heard Redd voice, but I didn't open my eyes; I couldn't let her see me crying. The constant beeping sound made me open my eyes, I looked around for the source, it was Redd's cell phone. She had it plugged into the wall on the charger. I closed my eyes, but something told me to glance over,

I saw Blaque's name pop up. I picked the phone up.

"We ready Daddy, I told you she was pregnant, all the signs were there." She took a picture of my positive test results, which were on the table in between us.

"Good job Redd, I'm on my way," he replied back.

"Sneaky dirty bitch," I said to myself. I put her phone back and closed my eyes like I was before she left. Redd took her seat and grabbed her phone.

"Blaque on his way Kandiland."

I was vexed, I couldn't believe she sat there and acted like she didn't just sale me out. Redd was looking for some brownie points from Blaque. Redd was going to get hers, I knew Blaque was about to beat my ass, there was no way I could escape it. Redd would feel my wrath, after it was all said and done I thought to myself.

I was glazing out the window when Blaque pulled up.

"Blaque here Redd," I said. I waited for her to walk, and then I followed behind tossing the papers in the trash by the door before exiting. Blaque played it cool, he didn't ask any questions. That scared me, I preferred him to rant and rave. Curse me out, he was too clam, that wasn't like him, worry consumed me.

We got to the house, we weren't even in the driveway fully. I opened the door and got out, Blaque and Redd followed behind me.

I climbed the stairs, rushing towards my room, I had to pee. I came out the restroom, Blaque was seated on my bed Redd was sitting on her bed.

"Take a seat Kandi," Blaque said his voice still so calm.

"Redd, leave me and Kandi alone for a second."

"Why, this what she wants to see Blaque, give the bitch a show."

"What are you talking about Kandiland?" Redd asked, acting like she was clueless as to what was about to unfold.

"Don't play dumb with me bitch," I spat.

"What happened at the doctors Kandiland?" Blaque questioned.

"C'mon Blaque, let's not beat around the bush. I know your little red head already told you what happened."

"I didn't say anything to him, so you can hush with that shit," Redd fired back.

"Bitch I saw your phone and the picture you took of my paper, you said I told you so. I'm glad I'm the topic of your conversation."

"Kandiland, girl you trippin' nobody have your name in they mouth."

"Redd just get the fuck out, before I fuck you up. You lying ass bitch," I sneered. I was beyond vexed that she wouldn't admit the truth.

"Redd go downstairs and don't let anyone come up here," Blaque said.
Redd stormed out the door, but not before I caught the glimpse of the grin on her face.

"So what happened at the doctors Kandiland?"

"Like I said before, your little red head already told you, that I was pregnant."
He sat there not saying a word. He stood to his feet and turned towards the door. I thought he was going for the door, until I felt his hand across my face.

"You can kill that motherfuckin' attitude, so you out here fuckin' these tricks raw huh?"

"I always use protection with everyone except you. I may be a hoe, but nasty is what I am not. I don't know what they have, why would I fuck them raw?"

"You fuckin' someone then. Who you fucking for free then?" Using his fist, he punched me in my face. "And don't you lie bitch, the truth gon' come out."
I didn't say anything; I would never give Moe up.

"You can't hear me bitch?" Blaque was pissed.

"I've been fuckin' ya' daddy bitch" I spat.

"So you got jokes huh?" Blaque smacked me. "Answer me, you have jokes?"

"Fuck you," I said. I knew I was making the beating worst, but I was fed up. I was fed up with being a punching bag.

"You like fuckin' tricks without any condoms huh? I might as well sell your ass to the Mexican Cartel and let them pimp ya' ass. Since you so damn nasty." Blaque continued to punch me, I curled up in the fetal position; trying to block the swings to my face. He grabbed me by my hair so he could look at my face.

"I told you before; I'm the only nigga that you can fuck for free and raw. Now I gotta have yo' funky ass tested."

Blaque delivered a two piece combo to my face, sending me crashing into the ground. Using his foot, he kicked me repeatedly in the stomach. "You don't have to worry about an abortion bitch, I just gave you one. That little creature can't survive that ass whipping." Blaque was tired he stood up not paying me any attention. I used all my might and grabbed his legs, making him fall. I stood up in so much pain and tried to make a beeline to the door. I ran right into Moe's chest.

"What the fuck is going on?" Moe asked gripping me by my arm.

"Move, this motherfucka' tryna' kill me," I blurted trying to push pass Moe.

Blaque had quickly gained his balance and was back on his feet.

"Where you think you going bitch?" Blaque gripped my hair, throwing me like a rag doll on the bed.

"Blaque let her go, what the fuck" Moe said jumping in Blaque's path.

"Leave little bro', this between me and this bitch."

"Nah, I can't do that. You gon' kill her."

"I might, if this bitch keep disrespecting me."

"I'm not gon' let you kill her."

"So you taking up for this hoe over me; you my fuckin' blood. To think about it, you always taking up for this bitch; you fuckin' my bitch? Is that yo' baby bro'?" Blaque questioned, pointing his gun at Moe. "You fuckin' my bitch little nigga?"

Moe was vexed. "You need to calm the fuck down nigga, and take that gun out my face, unless you gon' use it today." Moe said not backing down.

"I'm gon' let you save her ass today, but you and that bitch remember, she belongs to me. If I can't keep her, nobody is going to have her." Blaque stormed out the room.

"You okay Kandi?" Moe questioned. He picked me up from the floor, carrying me like a newborn baby, he ran down the stairs. The girls looked on in concern, but scared to ask.

Last thing I remembered, I was in Moe's arms, when I woke up, I was in the hospital. Once again, I laid in the hospital from the hands of another man.

"Hey Kandi," I heard a females voice say. I looked around, it was Shae. "How are you feeling?"

"Hey," my raspy voice was low and dry.

"It's okay, don't try and talk. I'm just glad you can open your eyes a little. That black motherfucka' put a beat down on you."
Shae took a mirror from out her purse, to show me my face. I had two black eyes and a busted lip.

"I heard what went down Kandi, its apart of the game. So don't think that you did anything wrong. He could have handled it better though. He was just mad, I've seen Blaque around for years, and there is something about you. I've never really seen him so mad about one of his hoes in his stable. You shot his ego down, getting knocked up by another man, and we all know he can't produce kids."
I sat there listening to Shae, I was in so much pain. My body hurt all over. I couldn't believe this had happened to me again.

"Kandi I'm in too deep, there is no turning back for me, but you can get away from this lifestyle. You still young and beautiful, you still have the chance to change your life around. Go make something out of yourself. You didn't choose this lifestyle, you were born into it. You're not addicted to any drugs, if you don't get out, you gon' be addicted to a man putting his hands on you. That's not the life you want."

"Why is it too late for you Diamond?" I chuckled calling Shae by her old working name.

"I use to be a Diamond, these days I'm just a rusty rhinestone. I used to be so vibrant, a brick house, but that was before the streets got a hold of me. Drugs were something I turned my nose up to, I would always say I would never be on drugs. Now if I can't get at least three hits a day, my day doesn't go right, I can't function without one," Shae chuckled. "I've been on these streets for twelve long years. I've been through several pimps, kidnapped, and contracted a few STD's. If a nigga don't smack me around, I feel that he weak, a bitch made nigga. I know people think I'm crazy, what kind of shit is that. After going from one abusive man to the next, the beatings get worst. You get accustom to the mind frame, you can't find better."

"I'm scared that I can't change, who is gon' love a bitch who sold her body for money?"

"You still young Kandi, you still have that spark about you to change. There will be a man that will love you for who you are, there is some men, who understand people make mistakes." Shae made me think of Moe, and the night of my birthday party, the words he said to me.

"Real men, will never judge a women for her past, especially if she has changed, and that life is just a thing of her past. But you worry about getting into school and finding a job. Make you some money that doesn't consist of you offering your body in exchange for it."

"So why can't you find a real man? Who won't judge you?"

"Girl please, nobody wants a crack addicted hoe hanging around, waiting to backslide and take everything that isn't tied down. Don't worry about me, I want you to get away from Blaque. I've seen many girls go missing. From the looks of the beating he gave you, if you stay I have a feeling a beating won't be the only thing he will deliver your way. And I don't want to see that happen to you, so get away from that monster. You know if you ever need a helping hand or advice you can call on me."

"Thanks Shae, you have always been real with me."

"And it will never change, but I'm gon' get out of here. You get you some rest. Remember what I said, get out Kandi, while you can, alive."

Shae walked out the door and in walked a nurse.

"I'm Nurse Jackie, I'm here to check your vitals. I will be your nurse for the night shift."

"Okay," I said to her.

"When you young girls gone stop letting these fools put they hands on you?"

"Can you just do your job and get out. Stay out of mine," I sneered. Pissed she was butting into my business.

"I was just tryna' give yo' young ass some words of wisdom, but let these young niggas keep putting they hands on you. I've seen many like you come through here, some don't make it out of here."

I had other things on my mind, than running all my business down to the nurse. I thought, but Nurse Jackie kept talking.

"What he was mad because you were pregnant? I know you were six weeks in, the way your ribs are fractured. I bet that was what he was trying to get rid of. It says you found out today. I don't see any track marks, so I know you're not on any drugs."

"Look lady, I'm good. If you knew what was best you would just leave it the fuck alone. You're barking up the wrong tree."

"I've been here many years and lived life that expands far back before you were even born. I've seen it all. I'm not an ounce scared of the shit you talking. I have survived drugs, an abusive husband and life on the streets, yo' tiny ass poses no threat to me." Nurse Jackie said making her way out of the room. In walked two detectives."Hello Miss. Timmons, I'm Officer West and this is my partner Officer Moreno."

"I don't have any information to give you," I said. I knew what they wanted and had no interest to give them anything.

"Well where were you when someone attacked you. They beat you pretty bad, we need a report so we can canvas the area, to see if there has been any other attack as vicious as yours."

"I was in Compton, can't remember the exact street, you know officer I can't even remember why I was there." I said to them.

"What can you remember?" Officer West asked.

"Not much, just getting my ass beat and you working my nerves asking all these damn questions."

"You look very familiar Miss. Timmons."

"I get that a lot officer; I guess I have a familiar face.

"Well if you remember anything, here is my card." The officer handed me the card. "Don't hesitate to give me a call, if anything comes to you."

"Yeah okay," I said to him.

The detectives turned and were preparing to exit the door, when they were met with Blaque and Moe.

"Well, well if it isn't the biggest punk ass nigga in California, the infamous Blaque." Officer West said.

"Officer West. How are you doing? How are your wife and daughter?" Blaque replied with a grin on his face.

"I'm good, family good. I would be better if we got low lives like you off of the streets." Blaque laughed. "I'm just a law abiding citizen, just like you officer."

"You're a piece of shit, and your day is coming Blaque, every dog has their day and so will you."

"Whatever you say officer," Blaque replied.

"How do you know the victim?"

"She is a friend of my little brother's," Blaque said pointing at Moe.
Officer West shifted his eyes from Blaque to Moe. His look said he didn't believe a word Blaque was saying. He walked closer to Blaque.

"Let me find out that you had anything to do with that girl being here. I will personally haul your punk ass off to jail."
Blaque smiled, "are we done here officer? Visiting is almost over and me and my brother want to check on his friend, we heard she took a pretty bad beating."
Officer stepped aside, letting Blaque and Moe into the room. "Blaque" he called out. "I got my eye on you."

"As you should officer, protect and serve is your job. Have a great night, I sure will" Blaque replied.

Once the officers were far from my room, Blaque marched close to my bed. "What the fuck you tell them?" His own tone had changed.

"I didn't tell them anything, I'm far from dumb."

"You better keep it like that, if you like your life."

"I know my role," I told him.

"You better play that motherfucka' like you trying to be nominated for an Oscar award for best supporting actress."

"Yeah okay," I said. I was glad Nurse Jackie walked in.

"I'm sorry gentleman, but visiting hours is over and she needs her rest."

"Well Nurse..." Blaque said eyeing her curvy body, looking for her name tag.

"Nurse Jackie is the name," she said.

"Nurse Jackie when will she be ready for discharge?"

"In a few days, we are waiting for her x-rays to come back, she took a bad beating. She needs time to heal, damn shame someone did this to her. They should be ashamed of their selves."

Blaque looked from Nurse Jackie to me, I didn't even look his way, and I know he thought I told her something. I told her to mind her damn business I thought to myself.

"Well we miss her already at home. And it is a damn shame what those girls did to her."

Nurse Jackie just looked at Blaque, the look on her face gave it away, and she was disgusted with him and saw right through his facade. She finished setting up my dinner.

"Well we gon' get out of here Kandi, you make a speedy recovery, and we need you at the house soon." I read between the lines. The look on his face told it all, than the kind words he spoke.

"Get well Kandi," Moe said giving me a slight smile.

Once they left out the room, big mouth Nurse Jackie started to run her mouth.

"So I take it, he is your pimp?"

"Didn't I tell you to mind your own fuckin' business, shit" I said. Nurse Jackie was meddling in something that didn't involve her, I didn't need the extra stress from Blaque.

"I could tell the way your body tensed up, he did this to you. He only came by to make sure you didn't talk. I was out there before, right after I left my abusive husband. I made my own money; I'm not knocking what you do neither am I judging you. Play it smart, it's your body getting used, while he out here shining and

spending money on the next bitch. If you gon'
sell your body, don't sell yourself short."

I lay there, hoping she would hurry up with
her rambling, she didn't know my life. How
could she give me advice and she didn't know
me or what I had been through. I thought to
myself blocking out Nurse Jackie, hoping the
medicine I was on, put me right off to sleep.

Chapter 19

I sat in the vanity mirror, as the make-up artist used light make-up to cover the bruises that still covered my face. It had been two weeks since I was released from the hospital. Blaque allowed me to rest my body once I was released, but after two weeks, I had to get back to the money.

I sat in the luxurious Beverly Hills Hotel, getting pampered for my date with the prime minster of Turks and Caicos, I didn't even know where that was, let alone how to pronounce it.

During The Players ball event, Blaque was introduced to the minster, who looked for high priced- escorts and prostitutes for events, I wasn't supposed to speak, unless the minster said so. He was to answer all questions for me. I was supposed to show up, get pampered, wearing evening gowns by designers I couldn't pronounce.

Most would be ecstatic to be in my shoes, to be wine and dined by a rich older man. For the first time in my life I looked at myself in the mirror and didn't like the reflection looking back at me.

Madam's words came rushing to me. *"Only the bad bitches make it off the blade, to the Hollywood Hills. There's power in pussy and I'm gon' show you how to use your power, to take you places out the ghetto."* At that moment, I declared I was tired, I didn't know how I would do it, where I would go, but I had to get away from this life, before it killed me, like so many girls before me.

"You all done," the Asian woman said. My make- up was flawless; the coral colored strapless dress was perfect. It looked like I was handpicked from a runway. Yet I was ready to give the minister what he wanted, a night of pleasure and be on my way.

I dressed and waited for the prime minster. He showed up to the room and looked me over.

"You are gorgeous." He said to me stroking the side of my face, I wanted to back away, I didn't like the gesture. I needed to be in Blaque's good grace, if I wanted to escape.

"I heard many great things about you Ms. Kandiland; I hope some of them are true."

I went into work mode. "Well we will have to see" I smiled.

The prime minster wasn't a bad looking man; he was tall, lean and had light salt and pepper hair. We made our way to the lower level, a car was waiting for us, and we got in. The minister didn't speak at all.

We pulled up to our destination; he got out first, then reached for my hand helping me out. We were lead into the venue. All eyes were on us, but I didn't feel special, I felt like everyone was staring and whispering at me.

The night went well; men flirted with me, their wives glared at me. The minister did all the talking amongst his peers.

When we made it back to the hotel, I was relieved that was over, but the night wasn't hardly over.

"Strip." The minster demanded.

I followed his demands and stripped down to nothing. He circled me, making a sound. He caressed me, like every other trick, I emotionally checked out.

He started to peel out of his clothes, I was surprised at his physiques, he was well built, and hung.

"Have you been drinking?"

"Yeah, I had a few cups of water."

"You're going to need more than that for this job," he laughed. I was confused I didn't know what he was talking about.

"What kind of job is this? I don't need a full bladder, to fuck you until you nut. I'm very skilled in that department."

"You just worry about getting some more liquids into your system, and let me worry about the rest," He laughed. "Go get whatever you want out the mini bar."
We were in the Presidential Wing, everything was all exclusive. I walked over to the mini bar and grabbed a cranberry juice; I opened it and took several sips from the bottle.

"You going to need more than that sugar." He said, taking a seat on the loveseat. "Try going into the restroom, turning the water on and sit there."
I made my way into the restroom; I turned on the faucet and took a seat on the toilet. The flowing water instantly made me feel the urge to pee.

"Do you have to pee yet?"

"How you know?"

"It works every time. Come... come," he said signaling me over.

"Stand over me," he said. He was sitting on the floor butt naked.
I stood over him, using his fingers he traced around my anal, inserting two of his fingers into my pussy.

"I have to pee" I said, making sure he knew. I wouldn't be able to hold it for too long.

"I know, don't worry just go."
Lapping his tongue on my vagina, sent an electric volt inside of me, causing my bladder to explode. Sending urine running down, he opened his mouth catching some on his tongue.

He used one hand to jerk on his penis, as the urine ran down his body.

"Yes, it's so warm" he shouted. Jerking on his penis harder, no sooner he was erupting like a volcano.

I was lost for words; I didn't know what kind of freaky stuff he was into.

"Grab that whip over there, I want you to spank me with it until I nut, okay."

"Okay," I said. I realized the more money they paid for your services, the crazier the things they requested.

I fulfilled his every demand; earning the ten thousand dollars Blaque was paid.

I was glad the night was over, I was ready to shower and lay down, and so much was on my mind. I hadn't talked to Moe since I was released from the hospital. I felt it was best; the pregnancy came too close to letting out our secret, I wasn't worth him losing the only family he had.

Chapter 20

It was like a breath of air, I woke up feeling good. I didn't know what it was, but I was loving it. I dressed and prepared for my day back on the blade, I was hoping to run into Moe. I just wanted to see his face.

I made it to the shopping center, it was flooded with working girls, money had to be flowing for the slay of women to be out, and visible.

"I see you doing better," Shae said.

"Hey Shae, yeah I'm good."

"I hope you remembered what we talked about Kandi."

"I heard every word Shae; it's not that easy to walk away from this life, it's all I know. But it's not what I want for myself, but I have to figure out what I want."

"I feel you, just don't take long to figure it out."

"I can't make any promises to you, but I damn sure gone try. I went on a date with a prime minster do you know he had me pee on him."

Shae laughed "Girl, the rich men be demanding some freaky shit, that's just downright nasty."

"His ass got a kick out of being spanked; the man actually busted a nut off me spanking him. That's some freaky crazy shit."

"The mo' money they pay, the freakier they play," Shae laughed.

"Aye Kandiland, some dude in a black truck been driving around looking for you, this the third time this week." Redd said.

"Did he give a name?"

"Nah, he didn't, just keep come by."

"Thanks Redd," I said.

I had just finished with a trick when I saw the all black truck with tinted windows circle the block. I had my eyes on the truck, until it bent a corner and was out of my view. I didn't know who was looking for me and what they wanted.

I wanted to give Blaque a heads up in case it was a pimp, trying to court me. But if he wasn't, he wouldn't care and I didn't have time to hear his mouth.

I decided to text Moe instead, and let him know what was going on.

I was making my way towards the mini mart to get something to drink, when the black truck pulled alongside the curb. The windows were tinted, so I couldn't see who was in the car. The window rolled down, I locked eyes with the man behind the wheel, it was him.

"Get in," he demanded.

I stood in disbelief, this felt like a fairytale.

"Get in Kandi," he said again.

I opened the door and climbed inside of the truck. I didn't speak, I was at a loss for words.

"How you been?" He asked.

"Surviving and living life, if that's what you call it. What about you, how you been?"

"I've been good, depending on how you look at it. I see you still out here on these streets?"

I was baffled he came at me like that. "Kris what the fuck did you expect? Do you know all the shit I went through when you left? How they starved me, left me in the house for days? I cried for three fuckin' days straight when you left, I didn't eat, I didn't move from the floor, for three fuckin' days." I was pissed he had the nerve to come at me like I was left in a better predicament. "Every year on our birthday, I cry and try not to stress, because I don't know whether you're alive, dead or in jail. Why didn't you come looking for me? Am I not good enough for you either?" Speaking with Kris brought out so many emotions in me. The beatings I took from Big, from Madam, Ice and Blaque. They all came crashing down on me.

"I'm sorry Kandi, I really am. I never meant to just up and leave you behind. I watched that house for days, wanting to run inside and save you, but I couldn't muster up enough courage. I didn't have shit to offer you, I was homeless and huslin' night and day, that was no life for you to be tagging' along with me."

"But being forced to have sex with my own fuckin' daddy and selling my body for money was? I've been with so many men, I've lost count. My body has taken more beatings then a professional fighter."

"Kandi, I can't change what has happened in the past. I'm sorry for all the hurt you have been through, I'm sorry I wasn't there to protect you. I'm sorry it took so long for me to come back for you, it was never my intention for it to be this long; but I got my shit in order now. I'm here for you now, I want that relationship we had back when we were younger."

I didn't know what to say. I hadn't expected to be so angry when I saw him. I stared at him, we were the spitting image of each other, just different shades, but when I looked at him. I didn't see me, I saw Madam. And for some reason that angered me.

"I look at you, and I see her. I've yearned for you since the day you left. I never intended to be so angry with you, I have been through so much bullshit in the last few years. I felt betrayed by you, you left me. You were my best friend, my ace. You left me for dead, leaving me in the hands of Big and Madam."

"I can never tell you how sorry I am Kandi, I truly am. Where have you been staying?" He asked. I watched him look at my arms; I knew he was looking for track marks.

"I'm not on drugs Kris. I have adapted to life on the streets, and being good at what I do. Taking care of myself, but besides weed I don't do drugs. I work for a pimp named Blaque, I stay in one of the houses he runs."

"Is that the dude you were at the player's ball with?"

"You saw me at the player's ball? I wanted to come up to you once I saw you on the stage, but you know."

"Yeah I understand, but I saw you, I didn't know if it was you for a fact, but my heart told me it was. When I ran into Big bitch ass with his two groupies, he confirmed it was you. He was looking for you, for a stunt you pulled." Kris had become angry speaking of Big, I could tell by his facial expression and the tone in his voice."I wanted to body that nigga, in that club where he stood, he grinned talking about how you would be his whether he got you dead or alive." Kris stated.

"Fuck Big and his two bitches," I spat.

"I don't care about them right now, in due time they will get what they got coming. Right now you are my only concern, so what's it gon' be sis'? I have enough money stashed away, to help you with whatever you need; to get away from these fucked up streets."

"Okay, I want to be done with these streets, but it can't be today." I stated.

"And why in the fuck is that?"

"Because I can't Kris, not today."

"Okay, I'm going out of town for a week; I hope you are ready by then. If you are not, I will drag you away from here myself. I will gladly body any nigga who tries to stand in my way,"

Kris sneered. His high pitch raspy voice raised, I knew he was telling the truth.

"Okay Kris."

"You are my sister, I will do everything I can to protect you, today forward."

"I hear you Kris."

"So do whatever you have to do, I love you Kandi; and I will see you in one week."

I paused, I hadn't spoken those words in so long, and it felt like it was foreign.I looked at him, "I love you too Kris."

I jumped out of Kris truck and watched him speed off; I hadn't paid attention to my surroundings. I felt a strong push from behind. I caught my body right before my body hit the Mini Marts glass window. I was vexed someone was pushing up on me from behind.

"You better watch it Kandiland," it was Honey.

"Fuck you bitch," I spat mushing her in her face.

"You been sitting in that car for a while, I hope you made some money. Tulsa wants you." She hissed with a smile on her face, pointing towards the direction she had just come from. I knew she was up to something, by the grin on her face.

I hadn't crossed paths with Tulsa in over a month. I knew he was pissed, which didn't bother me much.

"Fuck you and that limp dick bastard," I spat. I wrapped my hands around her neck banging her head into the glass window. "Yo' ass don't have much to say now, do you?" I gripped tighter around her neck.

"I hope he beat yo' ass bitch," Honey hissed spitting into my face. I blacked out, I removed my hands from around her neck. I began to throw blows at her face, blow for blow. She was bleeding, but that didn't stop me.

"Now who getting they ass beat, bitch!" I spat. Throwing more blows at her.

A small crowd started to form around us, I could hear Officer Tulsa yelling. I didn't care.

"Break it up ladies, before I arrest both of you Tulsa shouted. Squeezing his pudgy frame in between us.

"I said brake it the fuck up, before I mace you bitches."

I let go of Honey's hair, which was filled with blood.

"This not over Kandiland," Honey yelled.

"Let me know when you ready to get your ass beat again." I yelled back at her.

"Let's clear it out, it's nothing to see people, go back to what you are doing." Tulsa said.

I started to walk off, while Tulsa was pre-occupied with clearing the parking lot out.

"Kandiland wait. I need to speak with you."

"Fuck you Tulsa," I said picking up my pace.

I was half way down the alley, when Tulsa pulled up.

"Get in Kandiland."

"Tulsa, I'm in a rush, I will get with you later."

"That wasn't an option, hop in now, because if I have to get out; I'm gon' finish what Honey couldn't do."

I stood in the alley, constipating if I should go with him or not, I knew he was gon' beat me like always, what was the use in making it easy.

"Like I said, I will be back I have some where to be." I continued to walk.

Tulsa, rode alongside of me, talking crap like always. I planned to make a beeline once I got closer to the motel, I knew Honey made it before me.

I was close to the Motel, when Tulsa cut me off, jumping out.

"So you was just gon' ignore my demands?" He questioned, backing me up against the wall.

"I told you I have somewhere to be."

"Yeah showering my dick with some love, I heard yo' ass was knocked up."

"I don't know what you talking about."

"Don't lie to me, the red head chick told me, right after I fucked her. You better watch out, her pussy a little tighter than yours is now." He said gripping me by my neck.

"Well go fuckin' harass her, and leave me alone."

"I want some of that sweet Kandiland, Honey wasn't enough. So open up, and let my dick get wet."

"I'm on my period." I said, hoping he would give up.

"A little blood on my dick won't hurt, now spread them. If I have to take it, I'm gon' fuck you anal, with no damn lube bitch." He spat.

I spread my legs and let Tulsa have his way with me.

"See that wasn't so hard, now was it?"

"It was horrible," I spat walking off.

"See you always have to open that fuckin' big mouth of yours." Tulsa said grabbing me by my hair from behind. "Some time you should just hush your fukin' mouth."

"Freedom of speech."

"You're a hoe, freedom of speech doesn't apply to you."

"And you're a fat fuck, who can't get any pussy, so you harass us hoes for free sex."

Tulsa didn't say anything; he gripped my hair harder, slamming my head into his squad car.

"What you say?"

"Kandiland you okay?" I heard a male voice say.

"Get the fuck away from here, before I arrest your ass," Tulsa shouted.

"Fuck you cracker ass pig, Kandiland you good? Do you need me to go get Blaque for this cracker?"

"Yes," I yelled.

That pissed the already vexed Tulsa off; he started throwing punches at me.

I could hear feet approaching. "Get yo' hands off of her you pussy ass cracker." The man shouted.

"You gon' shoot me nigger, huh? Over this hoe," Tulsa said flinging my body to the ground. My vision was blurred, I thought I saw Bone.

"I'm the fuckin' law son, shoot me, the whole city of Compton will be looking for your low life ass."

"Kandiland, get up and make a run for it" Bone said. I struggled to get to my feet, my vision was still blurred, my head was banging.

"Kandiland don't listen to this nigger, you better stay your ass on that fuckin' ground." Tulsa shouted.

"RUN KANDI," Bone yelled. Shaking holding the gun close to Tulsa.
Tulsa saw the fear in Bone; using the opportunity, he punched him. Bone staggered, but didn't fall.

"Fuck you," Bone yelled pulling the trigger, but no bullet came out, the gun jammed.

"Looks like we have a problem." Tulsa chuckled, whipping out his pistol and painting several shots into Bones body.
I screamed watching Bone's dead body hit the ground. I could hear Tulsa calling the shooting in, I ran. I ran until I made it to the motel that was less then 50 feet away on the other side of the alley.
Moe was standing outside of the room."Kandi, what's wrong? Where is that blood coming from on you?" He asked in a panic.

"It's not mine, its Honey's. We got into a fight not that long ago.

"Where did those shots come from?" He asked looking me over, for any wounds.

"He killed him."

"Who killed who?"

"Officer Tulsa, he killed Bone, right in front of me."
I cried, "He was trying to save me, I got him killed." I cried harder. Bone would have still been alive if he didn't try and save me.

"Get in the car, lets get you away from here" Moe said, putting me in his car.
We passed by the alley, the ambulance had the area blocked off, and Bone's dead body was still laying on the floor covered up.
The ride to the house was quiet; I was lost in my own world.

"He has to die."

"What? Who?"

"Tulsa has to die, we can't breathe the same air."

"Kandi let Blaque handle that, keep your hands clean. Blaque has people who can take care of that." Moe said trying to reason with me, but my mind was already made up; Tulsa was going to die.

"When? Blaque been saying that shit, yet Tulsa is still beating my ass, fucking me when he wants and how he wants. Blaque don't give a fuck about me, just the money I make for his black ass," viciously I yelled.

"I know you're mad, but that's a cop. You can't just kill him and get away with it little mama."

"Watch me," I said.

Moe didn't say anything else the rest of the ride. When we pulled up to the house, I slammed his door and rushed into the house.

I needed a shower, Honey's blood had dried up on my clothes and skin.

When I came out the bathroom, Moe was sitting on my bed.

"Thanks for the ride, I don't need a baby sitter, I'm good." I said to him, hoping he would get the hint that I didn't want to be bothered with him.

"I will help you with whatever you need, just make sure it's planned out Kandi. I know he has caused you a lot of pain. I know you were still going to do it regardless. I'm out, get some rest little mama." Moe said, kissing my lips. I kissed his lips back; I missed the feel of his lips.

"Thank you Moe."

"Thank me when it's all over. I will tell Blaque what happened, and that you weren't feeling good."

"Okay."

I watched Moe walk out; I wish he didn't have to go. I pulled out my stash once I heard Moe's car pull out the drive way. I counted the money, adding what I had in my purse to it. I put it back and lay down, falling fast asleep.

Chapter 21

Kris was due back in town in two days, I wasn't any closer from departing from the streets. I couldn't make a safe departure, with some people still living. I would always have to look over my shoulder; I didn't want that.

Blaque dropped us off, and like always he was ranting his normal bullshit, that I didn't care about.

As soon as I saw his truck pull off, I went the opposite direction. I made my way to the pawnshop down the street. I looked around, looking for the perfect weapon; I needed something small but able to do the job.

I picked out a pocketknife and was back out the door, I couldn't be unseen for too long, the eyes were watching and ready to report.

I made my way back to the blade, taking a few dates. I waited on Moe's text, for me to meet him at the motel. I saw Tulsa, driving up and down the street; he had another officer in the car with him. I was thankful; I knew he wouldn't harass me, with another cop riding along.

It was perfect timing, I got the text from Moe. The coast was clear Blaque had finally left. I took the back streets to the motel. Moe was sitting on the bed when I entered the room.

"So you have this planned out little mama?"

"Yes, every Thursday Tulsa and I go to this apartment complex, where fiends hang out sometimes. We go up at different times, which will give me time to do what I have to do before he gets up there."

"Okay, and what if he just wants it in the car?"

"I know Tulsa, he feels it's more intimate in a bed. For months this has been the routine we have had. I will text you when I get into the car with him, so you can wait for me."

"You sure you got this?"

"I got this, it would be easier for me, and he won't expect it. I just need you to pick me up and cover if someone asks where I was when it happened. Everyone knows Tulsa and I have a past."

"I got you Kandi, I just want you to be safe. He is a cop. Do any fiends hang out regularly there?" Moe questioned.

"Not really. It's in the hood, the police won't respond that fast, if you are in place once I'm done, we will be long gone when they do show up. The police will be thick, when they do finally come, since he is a cop." I said to Moe.

"Okay, well I don't want you to get in trouble, Blaque should be back any minute. He just went to pick up some money."

"Okay, thanks Moe for helping me."

"You know it ain't nothing, but you have to do something for me."

"What's that?" I asked.

"Get away from my brother before he kills you," Moe said. It was the way he said it, that made me feel like; he knew something that I didn't.

"I plan to," I said with a shy grin on my face.

"Good, enjoy the rest of your night."

I walked out the room, feeling a little better. I wanted Tulsa dead for unselfish reasons, for every woman he beat and raped, because he could.

The night passed quickly, traffic was steady making it a breeze. I made my minimum and was off to sleep mentally preparing for what I had planned.

Chapter 22

I woke up, today I didn't feel the same, it was like a whole 360 turn. I looked at myself in the mirror, I saw a different person. Sweet revenge consumed me, all my life I sat and let people run over me, today that would change.

I could hear Blaque laying on his horn for us to come outside. I made sure everything I needed was in my bag, I grabbed it and made my way out the house.

"What's good Kandiland?" Blaque asked when I got into the car.

"What's good?" I replied dryly.

"What the fuck is wrong with you? You better fix that attitude, I don't want no shit out of you today" Blaque stated.

"Nothing, I'm good. There won't be no shit out of me, as long as bitches stay in their lane," I said.

"Lose the fuckin' attitude bitch," Blaque spat.

I wanted to yell, you're my fuckin' problem you black piece of shit. But I didn't, I just sat back, hoping the ride didn't take long; I had other things on my mind.

"I'm good daddy," I said this time my voice a little calmer, a wicked grin plastered on my face.

"That's more like it" Blaque said, turning the music up. I sat back and thought of the act I was about to commit. The black hawk rigged knife was tucked in the secret stash in my purse. We pulled into the shopping center Redd and I got out of the truck. Shae and Honey and a few other chicks were standing up against the wall.

"What's good?" I asked.

"What's good Kandiland?" Shae asked.

"What the blade looking like?" I asked no one in particular.

"It's cool, traffic has been steady." Shae said.

"So you don't see anybody, but Shae" Honey spat with an attitude. I ignored her, letting her question roll off my back.

"Has anyone came looking for me?"

"Yeah that nigga in that Lexus, the old dude." Shae said.

"Thanks, hit me if he come back."

"Well fuck you too bitch," Honey spat viciously.

"Nah bitch, I only fuck stiff hard dicks, when the price is right. You know I don't like your ass, so cut the bullshit; unless you want me to finish that ass whipping." I sneered glaring at Honey, waiting to see if she made a certain move.

"Whatever!" Honey replied, her eyes hawked me, like she wanted to bring harm my way.

"Just stay out my way because you don't want it," I said brushing past her.

"Is that a threat?" Honey hissed, looking me up and down.

"It's a promise, and you can run and tell Blaque that too, snitch ass bitch." I blurted making my way to one of my tricks cars, I spotted him from a distance.

I found it to be funny, that many talked down about prostitution and belittled the women who were in the lifestyle. Yet, I had police officers, politician and even the mayor; as regulars. They paid top dollar, to discreetly sex me any way they wanted.

I slid into the Lexus with Councilman Steve Calhoun, he drove off. I wanted to speed up the process, so I unzipped his pants and let his harden member sprang up, sliding the condom on, I handled my business.

It took a little over an hour to service Steve. He drove me back to the blade, using the back streets. As we pulled into the parking lot, I spotted Honey alongside the trash bin with a trick.

"You can let me out here," I said to Steve.

"Okay Kandiland, see you next week." Steve said, sliding the envelope full of hundreds my way. I took the envelope with the wad of money and stuffed it into my bag.

I stepped out the car lightly closing it, trying not to make much noise. I hid behind the brick wall discreetly, trying not to be seen by Honey or the chubby man she was servicing. I slid the baseball cap onto my head and put the gloves on. I slid the knife into my hand.

I patiently waited until they were done. I waited a few more moments watching the trick until he was in enough distance, to not hear Honey if she yelled.

Honey's back was towards me, as she squatted cleaning herself. I crept up behind her, not trying to startle her. I covered her mouth first, trying to muffle any screams.

"See bitch, you should have just stayed quiet and minded your fuckin' business." I whispered into her ear, letting the blade effortless slide on her neck, I didn't apply too much pressure. Her skin ripped easy, her blood squirted out. Her eyes rolled back, as she took her last breath.

Her blood covered my shirt. I laid her body behind the dumpster, quickly taking the blood drenched shirt off, throwing it into my bag and rushing off. I rushed into the swap meet to get a clean shirt.

When I walked out the swap meet, I saw Tulsa squad car parked. I stopped, and sent Moe a text letting him know I was about to get into the car with Tulsa. I waited for Moe's reply before making my way to Tulsa car.

We arrived to the tiny ran down apartment complex. Gang graffiti covered the dirty walls. The apartment was owned by one of the base heads; Tulsa harassed.

We never went in at the same time, which worked perfect for me on this particular day. I went in first, I hurried up the stairs, and I slid the knife under a stack of papers on the night stand for easy access. I ran into the rest room, I knew he would be upstairs in any minute; I needed to make sure he was comfortable.

I heard his deep breaths, and heavy feet. "Kandiland where you at?" He called out.

"In the restroom, strip and be ready for me" I said hoping he did.

"Hurry the fuck up, I'm on duty."

I waited a few more minutes, I could hear him huffing and puffing, while trying to free himself from his clothes.

I walked out the bathroom, Tulsa was on the twin bed bare naked. Just like I expected, his service weapon was lying on the night stand next to him. I didn't make a sound as I walked closer to him, my eyes glued on the gun.

"KANDI!" he yelled loudly. "Hurry the fuck up bitch."

I grabbed the gun "I'm here baby" I said pointing the gun at him. He laid there, eyes still closed. Waiting to slide inside of me and fuck me any way he wanted and not pay me. Take my money and beat me, this shit would end now I thought to myself. The power I felt, holding that gun sent a smile on my face.

Tulsa opened his eyes ready to spaz on me, when he got the shock of his life.

"Bitch, what the fuck are you doing?" He asked, I could hear the fear in his voice.

"What the fuck it look like motherfucka'?"

"So you gon' kill me now, I'm a fuckin' cop. They will bury your ass under the jail."

"First, they have to catch me, and even if they do. I will take that to get rid of you, you piece of shit" I spat.

"You don't have enough heart to kill me," Tulsa hissed trying to taunt me.

I started to laugh, mischievously. "All the shit you put me through, all the beatings, rapes. I hope your fat ass made peace with your maker," I said firing a round into his body, then another one and another one. I grabbed the knife and plunged it into his chest, repeatedly. Flashbacks of all the times he raped me, slapped me around. Before I knew it, the bed and Tulsa was covered in blood.

I grabbed my shirt cleaning the blood off of me, I dashed out the house and down the stairs, in nothing but my boy shorts and bra. I saw Moe's car parked on the corner, I scanned the area making sure no one was around looking. There wasn't anyone, I rushed to Moe's car.

I knew it would take some time for the police to respond to the gun shots, the area was stricken with crime. Gun shots were like the Mexican lady screaming tamales on a Saturday morning.

Moe didn't speak, just took off. I watched him scan me over, looking for any wounds. We made it to the Spot, Moe went to make sure the room was clear.

He came back out, waving me in. I hurried inside and stripped, rushing to shower and wash all of the blood, off my skin.

Moe was seated on the bed waiting for me."How are you feeling?"

"Fine, I thought I would feel different, but I feel the same" I said. Tulsa couldn't hurt me anymore, yet that wasn't enough for me. Honey couldn't tell on me anymore, yet it wasn't enough for me. I wanted them all dead, I was tired of all of them and they all had to die, I thought to myself.

"Kandi, are you sure you okay?" Moe asked, I could tell from the look on his face, he didn't believe me that I was okay.

"I killed Honey," I blurted out.

"What?" Moe asked jumping up from the bed.

"Honey, I killed her today." I said calmly. I know I sounded crazy, I should've felt remorseful, I ended someone's life, but I didn't. I was ready to commit murder again.

"Kandi, that wasn't a part of the plan. Do you know you just made yourself a suspect? You are known for having issues with both of them. Tulsa was a police, they are going to ask around, ask questions. You know, as well as I do, these chicks don't like you. They won't hesitate to give your name" Moe yelled, he was vexed and pacing the floor. He had never raised his voice at me.

"I don't care?" I hissed, pissed that he didn't see my point of view.

"What the fuck you mean you don't care? This isn't just your fuckin' life you playing with," Moe snapped.

"You didn't have anything to do with it," I said to him.

"Still Kandi, that wasn't a part of the plan, that was sloppy. You need to dress and make yourself seen, so people won't connect the dots."

I didn't respond. I just slid into the extra clothes I had and left the room without even saying anything else to Moe.

The blade was so busy, it seemed no one even noticed that I was missing. I fell right into line, flagging down cars. I was on a high, taking someone's life, made me feel on top of the world, it gave me a rush I had never felt before, and for some reason I liked it.

Chapter 23

I woke up early to catch the channel 7 news, I didn't watch the news much. I was looking for a particular broadcasting. Before my shift was over last night, the police were thick, no one had said anything.

All the girls were home, so it was a lot of movement around me. As soon as I turned on the television, Honey's face was plastered on the screen. The headline read Prostitute Slang.

"The body of Samantha Ramirez was found dead late last night behind a dumpster in the 2300 block of Bullis Road. From the information we gathered, Ramirez was a known prostitute in the area, going by the name Honey.

We don't have any witnesses to the horrible homicide; the police are trying to locate the victim's family."

I sat a grin on my face, as I admired my handy work. *"Shouldn't have fucked with me"* I said to myself. Just as the thought popped into my head, Blaque and a few of the other girls walked into the living room. I put my poker face on; I already knew what the visit was regarding. I decided to start the conversation.

"Damn that shit is fucked up what happened to her" I said, inside I was smiling.

"Why do you care, you didn't even like her" one of the girls said, her and Honey were close.

"I sure in the fuck didn't, that doesn't mean I wanted to see the bitch get murdered and left behind a dumpster." I snapped.

"You probably happy Honey gone, so you can get all the attention." The girl snapped back.

"Bitch you must not really know me, Honey was no threat and neither are the rest of you hoes." I fired back, vexed that this hoe was stepping to me, on some I'm a hater type of bullshit.

"Cut it the fuck out, both of you," Blaque intervened.

"Her tired ass started it," I added sending Blaque over the edge. He grabbed me by my neck. "Didn't I say shut the fuck up, I got more shit on my mind. Then to hear you two hoes fussing, both of you hoes tired to me."

I just stared back at him; the look of fear was replaced with eyes full of hate, rage and revenge.

The look on his face, told me he could see a change, but couldn't place it.

He let his grip on my neck go. "I don't have time for this shit," He said.

I focused on the screen, as he mumbled about safety issues and how the police would be all over us.

I blocked out his voice, my mind was on other things. Kris was due back in town today, and I wasn't any closer to departing. Getting rid of Tulsa and Honey were only a piece of it.

Suddenly the room became quiet as breaking news flashed across the scene.

"Officers have been looking for Officer Peter Tulsa, since yesterday. The officer's body was found this morning in a building invested by drug addicts. The officer was found nude; he sustained several gun shots and stab wounds. The police are canvasing the area for any possible witnesses or suspects to this heinous crime against an officer of the law."

Blaque looked at the television "Someone got to that fat cracker before me." He then looked my way "it seems like someone, likes you. Two people you couldn't stand, killed in the same day."

I didn't acknowledge his statement.

"You bitches still have work to get to, get y'all asses up and get ready; Moe will be here in an hour." Blaque said walking out the door.

I dressed for the day, and waited for Moe to arrive. I was glad the other girls were in the car, so that Moe couldn't talk to me. I didn't want to hear the slay of questions he might ask.

When we arrived to the blade, the police was still thick; I couldn't see why they wanted us out here. I jumped out the car, not wanting him to ask to talk to me, and made my way towards the back of the shopping center. Traffic was slow no one wanted to be seen. I wandered down the back streets trying to stay out the way of the police and their line of questioning.

I could hear a car approaching, I turned around and it was Detective West, immediately I became nervous.

"Ms. Timmons, how are you doing this afternoon? Can I talk to you for a minute?"

"I'm fine, and nah, I got somewhere to go." I replied never looking his way.

"Just a few seconds, I see all of those ugly bruises finally cleared up off your beautiful face."

"Yeah they have."

"You still don't have any leads on who attacked you?"

"I told you in the hospital I didn't know, and it's still the same, I don't know." I snarled I was already agitated with his presence.

"I don't understand how such a pretty girl like you; has so many enemies?"

"I don't know officer, but are we done? Like I said I have somewhere to be."

"Well let me give you a ride."

"Nah, I'm good" I said, I wouldn't dare get into his car.

"You still look very familiar; do you happen to know a woman by the name of Erica?"

"Nah, everyone has a twin, maybe that's mine." I said to him hoping he would drive off.

"Or maybe your mother?" He said.

I turned and faced him; I know the expression on my face gave it away. He had hit it on the nail; I didn't know how he knew Madam and was trying to figure it out.

"Nope, that's not my mother's name. My parents were killed in a car accident five years ago."

"Okay, Ms. Timmons" he said, I knew by the way he said my name, he knew I was in fact Erica's daughter. "Tell Blaque I have my eye on him, and his days are numbered."

"Yeah, have great day officer" I said, hitting the corner swiftly walking away trying to put much distance between me and the officer.

I made my way back towards the blade, the police had started to clear out a little, and the traffic still hadn't picked up. I saw Kris's truck speeding towards me, I wanted to hide, but I knew he had already spotted me.

He stopped next to me. "Get in" he shouted over the loud music he was playing. I got into the car, thinking of lies to tell him.

"Hey I said."

"What's good? I see you still out here; do you enjoy this hoe shit?" He blurted.

I sat baffled by his outburst. "So that's how you feel about me?"

"I'm sorry, I didn't mean for it to come out like that, I just can't understand."

"There is a lot you won't understand, all I am saying is let me do me. I'm tired of these streets, of the beatings and the rapes. But when I depart from these streets; this time it will be for good." I said to him. I could feel the tears threatening to fall, I wouldn't let them. There was no longer room for crying, just for the inner rage that lived inside of me to be unleashed.

"It's that easy?"

"It's never easy, but sometimes what's best for you may not be easy. That's a chance I am willing to take."

"So what are you saying Kandi?" Kris asked. I could feel his eyes burning holes into the side of my face.

"I just need two more weeks; I have to make sure all loose ends are tied."

"I'm gon' give you these two weeks Kandi, but no longer than that. Like I told you one week ago, if I have to drag you away I will." Kris said, going under his seat and pulling out a gun. "I mean what I said Kandi, I will lay any and everyone who tries to stand in my way."

The look in Kris's eyes I knew he was speaking the truth; he wouldn't hesitate to kill anyone in his way. I thought about telling him to off Blaque, but I wouldn't get the justice I wanted, if I didn't do it myself.

"I need these two weeks, so there won't be anyone standing in my way, yours neither." I said to him, looking him straight in his eye, so he would believe my every word, because it was the truth.

"Okay, I will give you that; I'm not going to ask you what you are going to do. I'm just gon' say be safe, I'm only a call away."

"Thanks."

"But I'm gon' get myself from these parts of town, these niggas in the hub is grimy, back to south central for me" Kris said, looking around him, for anything that seemed off. "I love you Kandi, two weeks sis, that's all, make the best of it; tie those loose ends."

"I love you too Kris, and I am. It's a promise to myself and you." I got out of his car and watched him drive away. I knew I would have to be on my best behavior with Blaque. The Blvd. was still so dry, and it was making me beyond tired. I knew Blaque would like to see me on my A game, and I couldn't do that on a dry blade, with no tricks. I called Blaque to let him know, with the police being hot, no trick wanted to be seen, and I suggested another blade to tackle. I knew he would take the bait, he wasn't into losing money.

It took five minutes for Blaque to arrive, I along with all the other working girls, jumped inside.

We arrived on Fig, the traffic was jam packed, and tricks drove up and down the street signaling down the first working girl they could find. I jumped right into the mix, flagging down and jumping into cars. I had only a week to impress Blaque, and convince him I was the young girl he met a while ago. The one fueled by sex and the chase of the almighty dollar.

The night was filled with traffic, making time past fast, before I knew it, it was into the wee hours. Blaque had arrived, rounding the girls up for drop offs.

"I will be doing count and pick-ups tonight" Blaque said, when everyone was in the car.

Which worked for me, I didn't want to cross paths with Moe and needed some extra time with Blaque.

Redd and I were the last to be dropped off like always. I walked slower, so he could take Redd's count first. I knew what Redd was trying to do, she saw me talking to the cop and Kris, so I knew she wanted to share those words with him. She figured if she went first I would have to wait, what she didn't know was, that's what I wanted her to do. That would give me an ample amount of time, to see where his head was and how I could get back into his good graces.

It took Redd and Blaque close to ten minutes to finish the count, Redd stepped out the room, I caught the smirk on her face. I stepped into the room.

"Hey Daddy?" I said a wide grin on my face as I slid him the wad of cash from my purse.

"What's good Kandiland? Good call on the blade little shit."

"It's nothing, just looking for the best interest of you, oh and that detective from the hospital West was his name I believe, he pulled up on me." I said knowing Redd had already said something.

"I heard. What was he talking about?" He asked while counting the money.

"Just if I knew who attacked me, I told him my answer was the same from the day he spoke with me in the hospital, and told me to tell you he has his eyes on you, and your days are numbered."

"Fuck punk ass West; you just make sure that story never changes."

"I got this." I reinsured him.

"I sure hope so, who was the dude in the black truck? You have been seen in that car more than once in the recent weeks."

"Daddy?" I called out getting his attention. "Didn't I just hand you a wad of cash? That's a trick, that's being serviced and handing over cash."

"Okay, I'm just making sure, you stay in line, or you know what can come." He stated. I could read between the lines.

"Yeah I do, I just think people need to stay in their own lane."

"Just do you Kandiland and that means no bullshit, just getting money." Blaque said standing up preparing to walk out the door.

"That's how it's always been, I just think ya' little catty chicks make it something else."

"Like I said no bullshit Kandiland," he walked out the door and Redd walked in. I knew she was out there listening. *"Sneaky bitch!"* I said low.

I didn't confront her on her bullshit, at least not now. I needed Blaque on good terms with me. An argument with Redd would only set me back, so I bit my tongue and got ready for bed. I never uttered a word to Redd.

Chapter 24

Days had past, me and Blaque hadn't crossed paths, he had been laying low since he was brought in for questioning regarding Honey's and Officer Tulsa's murder. I didn't know how I would be able to pull off getting him alone. I hadn't seen Moe in weeks due to football season was in full affect, he was busy with that.

I got up and dressed for the day, Blaque had a new guy on board doing pick up's and drop offs. I waited for his call. I was taken back when I got a call from Blaque that he was picking people up today. Redd had already left for the day. I changed my outfit into something that was more Blaque's taste. I waited for him to arrive, when he did I pranced to his truck a wide smile on my face.

"What's good Kandiland, I see you in good mood, what's gotten into you."

"Hey Daddy, nothing I'm just in a good mood today. How about yourself?" I asked not giving two shits how he had been.

"I'm good, now that the fuckin' pigs not down a nigga back and shit. But what's really good with you? Cause you been on some other type of shit in the last few months?"

"It's just first it was Honey, then Redd came and you started to switch up on me. I thought I was yo' bottom bitch, the one getting your money off top, wads of it."

"It's nothing like that Kandiland the only thing I am loyal to is my money. A lot of you bitches jump ship, so I never just give a lot of attention to one woman, when I have a stable of bitch's to tend to. Your just another dollar sign to me, sorry to break it to you. You have always been my money maker, that never has changed, but yo' attitude is fucked up and I don't have time for that shit, so I beat yo' ass." Blaque hissed glaring at me. "I got you off the streets to the cream of the crop, you went on dates with Millionaires.

"My attitude is only a reflection off of the attitude being given to me," I hissed back. "So how about we start fresh, no bullshit, no drama."

"Show me with actions baby, not with your words. I need to see it in the flesh."

"Stop by the motel and I will show you how sorry I truly am" I smirked. When it came to sex, Blaque was always down with it.

Blaque smiled and I knew I had him, he never turned down sex, we hadn't engaged in sex in months, due to us being at odds.

Blaque sped the rest of the distance to the spot, ready to lay inside of my pussy. As soon as we stepped foot into the room, he dropped his pants to the floor. I pushed him on the bed. I did a little naught dance for him while stepping out of my clothes. Blaque was a fiend for pussy; he loved all kinds and shapes. White, black, brown or pink, he had to have it. Blaque needed sex, two or three times a day. It was early so I knew he may not have had any, unless he woke up in some. I knew all the right moves to do, to get him head over hills. I pulled his dick from his briefs; gently I pulled on his dick that had quickly begun to rise.

"Who does you best baby?" I asked seductively.

"Nobody does it like the Kandiland."

I began to tease his penis until he begged me to suck him sloppy like I knew he liked. I teased him more, I was in charge.

"C'mon Kandiland suck my dick, like you know I love it," he begged.

At that moment, for the very first time, I was grateful for Madam, and the skills she instilled in me. I gave him what he wanted, sloppy head filled with tons of saliva, lots of tongue and lip. I could feel his leg twitch, his toes must have curled, from the pleasurable sound that escaped his lips, and I knew I had him. His eyes were closed; he was lost in the rapture. I used this moment to remove the gun out of his holster, which was on the back of his pants. I gave his penis more attention, I knew he was on the verge of cumin' I felt his leg shake. I felt his strong arms grip my shoulder, then my body being slammed onto the bed. He pried my legs open; I felt a sensation, which made my body jerk. I felt my sweet juices began to flow. Blaque lapped his tongue on my pussy, savoring all of my juices. How he switched it up on me? I thought I was in control not him, I'm running this. Blaque was skilled with his tools, to cause any woman pleasure, it was the wicked lifestyle and the pain he brought with it, that most couldn't endure.

I thought to myself, what a waste of a man, he was skilled with his tongue, with his dick' but wasn't worth shit. Most women didn't have a man with good dick action, because those are the ones, who mistreat you, abuse you, pimp you. So they settle with mediocre dick, to keep them happy. I was done with him pleasing me; I wanted to give him his last taste of pussy. I thought to myself, looking down at his head deep in between my legs, I was willing to lose my life, to make sure he wouldn't walk out this room alive.

I swung my legs over his head, and got on all fours. Spreading my legs, waiting for him to slide behind me. He did, I let out a light moan, as he found his way inside of me. He wasted no time, digging deep, he rocked fast, harder, he dug deeper inside of me. He flipped me over, pent my legs behind my head, and dug deeper, he always loved that I was so flexible. I watched the beads of sweat cascade down his face.

"Umm" he moaned loudly. "I haven't been in my pussy in a while, ahh shit, you been letting someone fuck my pussy, huh?" He questioned digging so deep, I hollered out loudly.

"Come give Daddy a ride" he said to me, smacking my exposed ass cheeks.

He leaned up against the headboard, his penis sticking right up. I squatted over him, easing onto it. I started to wind my hips, gripping the head bored, I moved faster, I started to bounce, and he gripped my hips helping me. Just then I heard a knock at the door, we blocked it out, and kept going. The knock only got louder, someone was persistent I thought. I hope they would just leave, go away. I needed them to leave so I could finish my task, but they didn't, the banging got louder and louder. I rode him faster, trying to block out the consisting banging at the door.

"Get the fuck away from the door," Blaque shouted.

"Open this door, you black bastard." The person shouted back.

"Get away," Blaque shouted again.

"I know you in there, fuckin' a bitch Blaque," the voice yelled. I finally recognized it, it was Redd. A wide grin found its way on my face. I knew we weren't going to open the door, and if I did, Redd would be dead, just like I planned for Blaque to be.

I rode him faster, so he could moan louder, I made sure to make high pitch moans. I was more focused on pissing Redd off, then the actual sex; at that moment.

Redd began to kick the door, the loud moans she heard only fueled her; she was angry he was laying up in some pussy and ignoring her. She kicked and kicked harder. I knew in due time the door would come down. The motel was old and cheaply built, the door wasn't that strong.

"Fuck this pussy Daddy," I beamed loudly. Just then we heard the door crash in startling us, in walked the angry Redd, she was even more angry when she saw it was me, her eyes told me so.

"What the fuck you want bitch? Get the fuck out, if you not gon' join us, shit." Blaque said.

I smiled a mischievously grin, still winding my hips onto him. "Yes daddy! Yes!" I moaned, taunting Redd.

She couldn't take it any longer, she charged at us throwing wild punches, hitting both of us. I swung back; I have to get her off me I thought to myself. I need to get this gun, they gon' die, only if I can get to this gun. I hit her hard, sending her flying back; I jumped up off Blaque. I rushed to grab the gun, I pointed it at Redd as she struggled to get up on her feet. I saw another figure, a figure in the room. I turned and locked eyes with Moe. The look in his eyes showed he was disappointed in me, at that moment I didn't care any longer.

"Close the door Moe," I said to him.

"Kandi," he called out. "What are you doing?"

"Close the fuckin' door Moe" I yelled this time pointing the gun at him. Redd had only broke the lock. He quickly closed the door.

"What the fuck are you doing Kandi, where you get that damn gun from?" He asked calmly sitting up, not fazed at the gun I was waving.

"Don't worry about that motherfucka' just know it will be what ends your worthless life."

"You ain't gon' kill me, you love me."

"Ha" I laughed. "You must be high off that powder, to really believe that bullshit. I can't stand the ground your black ass walks on."

"Bitch I took you in, when your own people kicked you out, and that punk ass nigga Ice fucked over you. I made you into the person you are today bitch, and you wouldn't be shit without me," Blaque shouted.

"Well if you feel that way, good looking." I said with the gun still aimed at him.

"You mad Kandi? You want to kill somebody, then kill Redd." Blaque said pointing to Redd.

"WH-what?" Redd asked looking from Blaque to me.

"You mad at me because of Redd. So kill her."
I laughed at him. "You're my fuckin' problem. If Redd would have just stayed in her fuckin' lane and didn't try to be me, I wouldn't have had a problem with her."

"FUCK YOU KANDI" Redd yelled.

"I know yo' ass probably wants a taste of the Kandiland, but I don't dyke bitch."

"Blaque, I'm pregnant. You just gon' let her kill me and your baby?" Redd pleaded.
We all fell into laughter, at Redd's expense.

"Bitch, that motherfucka' can't have any kids, all he shooting is blanks" I snarled. "So you think, he beat the fuck out of me because I was pregnant with his child," I laughed. "Face reality boo-boo. Blaque is your pimp, not your man. Oh, so you thought y'all was gone be a happy little family?" I asked.

"So who were you pregnant by?" She asked. The look of confusion on her face, she didn't really understand everything going on around her.

"Moe," I said. Shocking both Blaque and Redd. Moe just dropped his head.

"You fucked my brother?" Blaque asked. I knew he was vexed, he always assumed but never was sure.

"Yup, and it was bomb I must admit. I didn't have to fake it, like I do with you," I said. It was a lie; I just wanted to bust his ego.
Blaque looked at Moe, with so much malice in his eyes. "You fucked my bitch bro'? I gave you any and everything and this how you repay me, fuck my hoe?"

"Nigga do you hear yourself? You gave me any and everything I wanted really? Just call it a small way to pay me back for the loss of my granny. Since it was your bullshit; which caused her death." Moe yelled.

"Honey wasn't lying about you two, the night of your birthday party?"
I smiled; he was finally connecting the dots. "That bitch should have kept her mouth closed,

and remained in her lane too. It's okay, I silenced her forever."

"You killed Honey? Didn't you?" Blaque tried to reach for his gun.

"You looking for this," I laughed. "Yeah I made sure to get it, see daddy, I already had this planned out."

Blaque just sat there; I knew he was trying to come up with a plan. He was trying to escape the death I was ready to deliver.

He studied the look on my face, I felt crazy. So I knew I had to look crazy. Redd watched me, when she felt I wasn't looking, she made a beeline towards the door, that was the wrong move. I squeezed the trigger, two shots flying from the gun, instantly killing her tiny body.

Moe and Blaque jumped, "Shit" Blaque said, lunging towards me. I fired a shot at him, sending him flying back towards the bed.

"It was nice knowing you motherfucka', now it's time you visit the rest of the dead." I fired three more shots into his body.

My heart was pumping; I loved the adrenaline I felt. Just like Officer Tulsa murder, I felt on top of the world, on a high.

I turned to face Moe, I didn't want to kill him, and I thought I was in love with him.

"I'm sorry Moe, I don't want to do this, but I have no other option."

"You don't have to do it Kandi, you don't."
He pleaded, I fired two shots into Moe. Blaque
was his brother, no matter what they went
through. He was his blood, he couldn't live.
I threw on my clothes, and rushed out the door. I
didn't check to see if anyone saw me, I had
plans to get far from these streets, far from this
city. I ran; I ran until I was out of breath. I sat
on the first bench I found. Once I caught my
breath I called Kris.

"I need your help, please come get me, I'm
thru, I'm done," I cried into the phone. I sat and
waited for Kris to arrive.
When Kris arrived, I rushed into his arms and
cried. I cried and he held me, rocked me, like he
did when we were kids.

"It's over, it's over." He said to me, putting
me into his car.

"It's not over Kris, not until Big and
Madam. Until they are dead, I can't live until
they are all dead." I yelled, tears still pouring
from my eyes.

Chapter 25

I got to Kris place, I showered and climbed into the bed and cried myself to sleep. I didn't cry because I committed murder, Blaque and Redd deserved to die in my book. It was Moe that affected me, he was always gentle, always kind. He loved me, and I think I loved him back. When I awoke, Kris was sitting next to the bed. He was watching me sleep, like he did when we were children; when I had first started working the blade.

"Hey."

"Hey," I said back to him.

"Kandi can I ask you something?"

"Sure," I said to him.

"Have you killed before?"

"Yeah, today made the second time in this month that I have killed." I replied.

"Are you prepared to end Big and Madam's life?"

"I was ready as a kid; to kill them."

"Well get some more rest, because we have a long night ahead of us." Kris said with a smile on his face.

"Kris what do you do for a living? This is a very nice place." I said admiring his home, it was more immaculate than the condo I shared with Ice.

"Let's just say, I am making the transition from a boy to a man. I'm letting go of all the foolish behavior and trying to build a future. I love music, and it's been a form of therapy for me, in my lyrics, I express the hurt and guilt I felt as a child."

"So you're a rapper?"

"Something of that sort, I'm not sure if it's something I see myself doing longevity, but I enjoy it and if my words can touch a young man or woman and give them enough courage to change, that's good enough for me."

"I feel you; I want to help people change. This life is wicked and it has taken many women under before my time, and will even long after me, but I want to help young girls. Help them not fall for men that mean them no good, like the men I have had in my life." I said to Kris, the faces of the men I encountered flashed before my eyes.

"You can do that Kandi, you can do anything you choose. But you have to get Kandi in order, before you can help the next. Get some more rest, you will need it." Kris said walking out the room.

I laid back down, thoughts swarmed my mind. Was this it for me, was this change going to be permanent. No more looking back, only forward.

"You got this Kandi, you are worthy of a normal life, outside of sex," I said to myself out loud.

It was into the wee hours, we had been sitting in the car for hours, watching the coming and going of this one particular house, Kris wouldn't tell me anything. He sat quietly, his eyes steady watching. I had never been on anything like this; I could tell he was accustomed to it.

"That's the last person that went in, that just left. Are you ready to finally put your past behind you?" Kris asked.

"Yes, I am." I replied. We were dressed in all black, fitted caps pulled down low over our eyes. We got out of the old van that Kris drove.

Slowly we approached the house, Kris handed me a gun, it was different from the ones I had saw before.

"You stay here Kandi, if anyone runs kill them. I am going to go through the back, and come open the door for you, but if anyone runs out before I do so, don't hesitate to blow they fuckin' brains out."

"Okay" I said.

Kris walked towards the back of the shabby house; it felt like forever, I started to get nervous. I could hear movement in the house, but no voices. I gripped the gun in my hand, prepared to deliver death to anyone who walked out that wasn't Kris.

The door knob turned, I aimed at the door. A sigh of relief overcame me when I saw it was Kris.

"Come on," he said looking around before closing the door behind us.

I walked into the house; Big, Madam and Starr were all sitting on the couch, their hands tied in front of them.

"Well, well if it isn't the ugly twins" Madam barked.

"Mommy dearest, are those the only words you have for your loving children? Especially since we will be the last faces you see."

"I see you finally did locate the hoe," Big spat, malice laced all over his words.

"Yo' bro' do these weak minded pieces of shits think that their words can hurt us now?"

"I assume, because they fail to realize, we are already broken, there isn't anything left for them to do to us."

We been broken; they had killed life inside of us as children. I want to be rebirthed, as an adult. They were the last piece of life, that I needed exchange for, so that I would be able to live my life.

They didn't say anything else; the mug on Big's face was priceless.

"I bet you never thought this would happen, right?" I asked that power was back, I was on a high.

"You don't have the heart to kill Kandiland, chill bitch," Big spat.

"My name is Kandi," I said. "No longer is there a Kandiland, that bitch died with the rest of them." I sneered.

"You were born a hoe, Kandiland will always be you. You're a natural at it, so word of advice, don't try to be someone you are not." Big barked.

"You know what, we didn't come here to talk, we came here to bury you motherfuckas' so we can live life. We are broken but not ruined, today we are born again." Kris hissed. Our guns rang off emptying the clip into their bodies. I looked to Kris, he looked at me. We looked at their bodies slumped over. Kris grabbed my hand and we walked out. Leaving the last chapter of our old life behind the door, dead with Big and Madam.

That night I smiled, because I knew my future was now in my hands. It was up to me to make the best decisions for my life.

Chapter 26

"Every saint has a past and every sinner has a future.
                              -Unknown

Dr. Gwen sat, and looked at me."Wow Kandi, you have been through a lot, but like I tell many women and men who come to see me, that's your testimony. So never be ashamed of what you been through, or where you been. If you did, you wouldn't be you and here now, knowing what you know." Dr. Gwen said.
A volt of relief shot through me. It was the very first time I had shared every detail of my life with someone.

        "So let's talk about your life now. You are married with two small children?"

"Yes I am. I've been married for four years now. Our son Karter is two and Kaila, our daughter is one."

"Does your husband know of your past? If so, how does he handle it?"

"Yes he does know of my past, because he lived most of it alongside of me."

"Huh? I don't understand Kandi?" Dr. .Gwen had a blank stare looking at me.

"Well it was about six months after everything happened. I had re-enrolled into school. I was walking from class and I could feel someone watching me, I looked around and saw no one. I continued to walk to my next class, when someone bumped into me, knocking my books out my hand.

"Let me help you pick those up." He said to me, I didn't see his face, just heard his voice. I gathered my books and stood up, finally my eyes connected with the kind man who helped me. I thought I saw a ghost, all color from my face, felt like it had drained. It was Moe, standing before me, in the flesh.

"It's okay Kandi, I am not going to harm you. I have been watching you all this week. I was scared to approach you, I didn't know how you would take it," He said. I was motionless, I was unable to speak.

"I shot you, shot you twice" I rambled.

"Yeah but the wounds didn't kill me" he said.

"I found out the shots didn't kill him. He crawled out the room, a man who was driving past, saw him and called for help."

"How does he feel about all of this?"

"For him, it's like déjà vu, his mother was a hoe, his father a pimp. I recently found out his mother, had dated his uncle first, who introduced her to prostitution. It was his father that killed his uncle because he had fallen in love with her."

"Okay, how are you two with your daughter Kaila?"

"We are very overprotective; my children don't attend daycare and will never. When it's time for school, they will be home schooled."

"Why do you think that is?"

"I'm scared for my children."

"From whom and from what?"

"Any and every one."

"Kandi, you haven't fully gotten over your old life, it's still hindering you today. You can't hold your children under you, because you are scared someone is going to harm them, because someone hurt you. You can't let the poor decision of your mothers; determine if you are a good mother to your children, neither if you are the perfect wife to your husband. Because those were Erica's bad choices, not Kandi's."

I couldn't help but let the tears flow from my eyes, as Dr.Gwen talked.

"I'M SCARED, SCARED I WILL TURN INTO HER," I yelled. "I'm afraid that it's a curse on my family that the cycle will repeat."

"Do you do any of those things Erica did to you, to Kaila?"

"No"

"Then the cycle isn't repeating. That cycle ended with you. Now it's time to live life. To be that strong mother to your children; that good wife to your husband. The time is here and now Kandi, like you said only moving forward."

"How do I move forward?"

"Forgive those who hurt you, as long as you are angry, they have the upper hand. Even in their deaths, they still haunt you. Forgive them, and ask God to forgiven them. Then forgive yourself, and ask God to forgive you."

Dr. Gwen scribbled on a piece of paper and handed it to me. "Tell the Pastor I sent you."

I looked at the paper; it was an address to a church. "Thank you Dr. Gwen" I said.

"No need to thank me, this is my job. Show me you are willing to move on. You are a strong woman; most don't make it out that life, alive and can survive all you endured. You are only as strong as you believe you are Kandi, I know you're very strong, but you have to realize that you are also."

Our time was up. In all the years of my life, with all the signs and advice that was given to me. Didn't mean much, Dr. Gwen's words touched me. I grabbed my purse and shook her hand. As I walked to my car, I knew it was finally time to release those demons inside of me. I wanted to live, live freely.

I picked up my kids, entered the address Dr. Gwen had given to me into my navigation and followed its directions. It didn't take me long to get to the church. It was a big brown building, a picture of Jesus on the front. It read New Faith United Methodists Church. I never been into a church before, my heart beat and my stomach fluttered.

"Mommy what is this place?" Karter asked.

"It's a church baby" I said to him. I knew he didn't know what that meant, I never spoke about God to my children, because I didn't know him myself.

I grabbed my children's hand and marched inside.

"Hello Ma'am may I help you?" A voice said behind me.

"Yes I am looking for a Pastor Troy Williams."

"I am Pastor Troy Williams, what can I do for you today Ma'am?"

"Dr. Gwen sent me over," I said to him.

"Are you in need of prayer sister?"

"I guess so; I'm in need of forgiveness."

"Well follow me this way." He said walking to the front of the church.

"I want you to kneel at the altar, I will pray out loud for you my sister, then you can say a personal prayer and leave it right here at this altar."

"Father God, I ask you to forgive this young woman for any sin she has committed. I ask you Father God to deliver her from any bad choices she has made. To forgive her from those demons that live inside of her. To forgive her for any harm she may have caused. She has come into your house Father God, to wash away her sins and to be forgiven Father God."

As he prayed he gripped my hand and prayed for me. I cried and for the very first time in my life, I felt Gods hands wrapped around me. I survived what I went through because he never left my side. I left my burdens at that altar.

"Thank you Pastor."

"Thank you, I will see you on Sunday at service?" He smiled.

"Yes, you will" I smiled back. I felt rejuvenated, alive and free. I stopped and looked into my children's eyes. God had forgiven me long ago, when he blessed me with those two heaven sent angels.

I made my way home, cooked, fed and bathed my children and I waited for my husband to get home from work.

When I shot Monty, I messed up a nerve in his arm. His chances of playing professional football went out the window. He was now the head coach for the Los Angeles own three time super bowl winning football team The Los Angeles Panthers.

When he walked through the door, I had his bath water and dinner waiting. When he was finished I made love to him until the sun rise.

Available May 20th 2014

Pre-order your copy today

Concreterosepub@gmail.com
www.NishaLanae.com